KT-399-614

LINCOLNSHIRE COUNTY COUNCIL
EDUCATION AND CULTURAL SERVICES.
This book should be returned on or before
the last date shown below.

SO2

SO2 6/02

AD 03332576

BRIDE BY CHOICE

BRIDE BY CHOICE

BY

LUCY GORDON

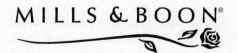

MILLS & BOON®

LINCOLNSHIRE
COUNTY COUNCIL

All the characters in this book have no existence outside the imagination of the author, and have no relation whatsoever to anyone bearing the same name or names. They are not even distantly inspired by any individual known or unknown to the author, and all the incidents are pure invention.

All Rights Reserved including the right of reproduction in whole or in part in any form. This edition is published by arrangement with Harlequin Enterprises II B.V. The text of this publication or any part thereof may not be reproduced or transmitted in any form or by any means, electronic or mechanical, including photocopying, recording, storage in an information retrieval system, or otherwise, without the written permission of the publisher.

MILLS & BOON and
MILLS & BOON with the Rose Device
are registered trademarks of the publisher.

First published in Great Britain 2001
Large Print edition 2002
Harlequin Mills & Boon Limited,
Eton House, 18-24 Paradise Road,
Richmond, Surrey TW9 1SR

© Lucy Gordon 2001

ISBN 0 263 17296 1

Set in Times Roman 16½ on 18 pt.
16-0502-46480

Printed and bound in Great Britain
by Antony Rowe Ltd, Chippenham, Wiltshire

PROLOGUE

'THEY'LL be calling you any minute,' Heather said, looking up at the screen that gave boarding details at Palermo Airport.

Lorenzo gave a sigh of pleased anticipation. 'Can't be soon enough for me. New York, here I come!'

'Well, try to remember what you're there for, little brother,' Renato reminded him. 'You're Lorenzo Martelli, Export Manager for Martelli Produce, visiting America to establish the firm in a big, new market; not Lorenzo Martelli, playboy, there to spend money enjoying yourself.'

'You can't stop him doing that,' Heather chuckled. 'But he might sell a few vegetables between orgies.'

She had to admit that her brother-in-law looked like a playboy. With his light brown curly hair, deep blue eyes, good-looking face, and athletic figure, he might have stood as a symbol of healthy, thoughtless young man-

5

hood: with the emphasis on ''thoughtless'', she decided with wry affection.

It was almost incredible that only a few months ago she had fancied herself in love with Lorenzo, had actually come out to Sicily to marry him, only to discover that her true love was his older brother Renato after all. Most women would have found her choice puzzling. Renato was a hard, difficult man who frowned more than he smiled, except for those he loved. Lorenzo had a smile for everyone, and was, in Renato's caustic words, 'too handsome for his own good or anyone else's'.

But Heather had seen beyond looks and discovered that it was the prickly Renato who touched her heart. She had been married to him for eight months now, and was expecting his child. It had been natural for the two of them to come to the airport to see ''their'' brother off to the States.

'Call us when you reach the Elroy Hotel,' Renato reminded him now. 'And don't forget—'

'Will you stop?' Lorenzo pleaded plaintively. 'What with your instructions and the list Mamma's given me of people to visit I shan't

have a moment to myself. She was so determined I shouldn't forget the Angolinis that she
called them yesterday, and the next thing I
knew I was promising to spend next Thursday
evening with them.'

'Our grandfather and Marco Angolino were
young men together before Marco emigrated
with his wife and son,' Renato reminded him.
'Their friendship was very close.'

'But that was years ago and Marco is dead,'
Lorenzo objected. 'I'm having dinner with the
son, who's now an old man, his wife, who's
an old woman, his three sons who are all older
than I am, and his four daughters, Elena,
Patrizia, Olivia, and Carlotta—all unmarried.'

The nervous way he said ''unmarried''
made Renato grin. 'In other words, you think
they're on the catch for you,' he said. 'Conceited oaf!' He aimed a friendly punch at his
brother's shoulder.

'Let's just say that the Angolinis are butch-
ers, and I feel as if I'm being laid out on the
slab for inspection,' Lorenzo observed gloom-
ily.

'Definitely you should marry one of those
girls,' Renato said, turning the screw with

brotherly malice. 'With their meat and our vegetables it's a match made in heaven.'

'Get lost,' Lorenzo told him without rancour.

The boarding call came. They all rose, and Lorenzo hugged his sister-in-law eagerly. Renato gave his brother the fierce, unembarrassed embrace of one Latin male to another.

'Behave yourself!' he barked. 'If you cause our mother a moment's anxiety I'll personally put an end to you. Now get going!'

As Lorenzo strode off, turning at the last minute to wave at them, Renato said, 'The annoying thing is that those daughters really will lay themselves out to trap him. Too many women do. That's his trouble.'

'Well, you know one woman who fell for you instead,' she reminded him, and knew, by the pressure of his hand, that she'd said what he needed to hear.

As they walked away she said, 'You're worried about him, aren't you? Don't be. He's a good salesman.'

'I know. I'm just bothered by the conviction that when he's in America he's going to go just that little bit too far.' He slipped an arm about his wife's shoulders. 'But it's too late to worry about that. Little brother's on his own now.'

CHAPTER ONE

SNOW was on the ground and a bitter wind cut through the darkness of an early February afternoon, but New York still glittered and nothing could dim the glory of Elroys, the most glamorous, the most expensive hotel on Park Avenue.

There was a new security man at the staff entrance, who didn't recognise Helen until she showed him her pass with its proud words, Helen Angolini, Management Trainee, and the even prouder words, ''First Class''. She'd joined a training program in which only one applicant out of a hundred was accepted, worked her way up from Third Class, through Second Class, and now she was on the last stage before a full appointment.

'Not that I'll ever get appointed if I'm late,' she groaned to herself as she dashed for the elevator to the eight floor. 'Can't this thing go any faster?'

'I didn't think you'd be here for this function at all,' said a voice beside her. It was Dilys, her fellow trainee, whom she'd overlooked in her agitation. They'd joined on the same day, soon become flatmates, and been ''partners in crime'' (as Dilys was fond of putting it) ever since. 'You've just gotten back from Boston,' she observed.

'Right, and I was supposed to be going straight to my parents' house from the airport. But Mr Dacre called and said to look in at the hotel first. That's why I've still got my luggage with me.'

At that moment the elevator doors opened, and Dilys grasped Helen's arm, steering her towards the ladies' room. 'Dump your things in here,' she said. 'And put your glad rags on.'

She was a petite blonde with a come-hither eye. Helen was taller, more statuesque, with shoulder-length hair as black as a raven's wing, and dark, expressive eyes. In her mid-twenties her lush beauty was reaching its height, but she thought her appearance reflected too accurately her Sicilian ancestry, and longed for blue eyes and fair skin.

Yet while she might disparage her looks she knew how to dress them to advantage. Her warm skin cried out for deep tones, and now she looked through her luggage until she found a dress of dark red silk that caused her eyes to glow theatrically. A vigorous brushing made her hair gleam and bounce richly about her shoulders.

Dilys regarded her with satisfaction. 'Great! Now let's go and knock 'em dead.'

'Don't you ever think of anything but men?' Helen chuckled, already knowing the answer. 'This is supposed to be a working function.'

'So? I like to mix business with pleasure. C'mon! Let's inspect the talent.'

The Imperial Room took up one corner of the eighth floor. On two sides it had floor-length windows hung with luxurious drapes. A dozen round tables groaned under food and wine. The huge room was already packed. All the big names of Elroys were there, and she could see Jack Dacre, her immediate superior, a hard taskmaster but with a kind heart. He signalled and edged towards her through the crowd.

'Glad you got here,' he rumbled above the din.

'My plane was delayed. I'm sorry I'm a bit—'

'No sweat. Tell me about your trip tomorrow. I've heard good things about your work while you were away. What do you know about this function?'

'Nothing. It wasn't even planned when I left.'

'Right. All thrown together at twenty-four hour's notice. It's the Continental Restaurant. The Italian section grew so popular that it's being hived off into a restaurant of its own. Most of the people here tonight are connected with food. Grab a drink.'

He vanished to do some mingling. Helen obtained a glass of light wine, and edged her way in the direction of Braden Fairley, the Managing Director. He was talking to a handsome giant with light brown, curly hair. Something in the way the young man was standing told Helen that it was taking all his good manners to seem attentive, but the expression of courteous interest on his face never wavered.

Then Fairley's attention was claimed by another guest, making him turn slightly, giving Helen a better view of the stranger just as he glanced up. Their eyes met. His, she noticed with pleasure, were deep blue and irresistibly merry. She couldn't help smiling back. He glanced at Fairley, blowing out his cheeks in a plea for sympathy, which she gave him willingly. Then the Managing Director resumed his monologue, and Helen moved along.

From beside her came a soft, appreciate growl. 'Mmm, he's yummy, isn't he?' Dilys murmured.

'Who's yummy?'

'Who's yummy? she asks, when she can't take her eyes off him!'

'I'm looking at Mr Fairley,' Helen said stiffly.

'Sure you are. Between Fairley and a guy who looks like a Greek god, you're going to look at Fairley. Who wants to waste time on a Greek god?'

'Don't be fanciful! Greek god! No way!'

'All right. Life-guard, then. I like that better. More chance of getting him where you want him.'

'I don't want him any way,' Helen said unconvincingly.

'Aw, c'mon! He must be six foot two, and look at those shoulders. They should build doors wider to let them through. There's no fat on him, you can see that, and with those long legs and flat stomach—well, if he isn't a life guard he ought to be.'

'You can't tell about his legs, or his stomach.'

'You can if you look properly,' Dilys chuckled. 'I glided by just now and he winked at me.'

'He looks as if he'd wink at anything in a skirt.'

'Hey, you noticed!' Dilys said with ironic admiration. 'And you should see the gleam in his eye! One look, and you just know he's scheming to take you to bed.'

'Oh, go away!' Helen said, laughing. 'Simply standing next to you could ruin my reputation.'

'See ya!' Dilys said, and slid away in search of more prey.

It was incredible, Helen thought, how her eyes seemed to be drawn to the handsome

young man of their own accord. She tried to
ignore him but she kept glancing back in his
direction without meaning to. And at last the
inevitable happened and she found him looking back. Embarrassed, she tried to assume an
air of lofty indifference, but somehow it turned
into a smile of pleasure because his presence
was like sunshine.

He was dressed informally but expensively
in slacks and a silk shirt, and Helen had to
admit that everything Dilys said had been true,
although 'Greek god' was a bit of an overstate-
ment, she thought, giving the matter serious
attention. But 'life-guard' definitely, and with
a look of relish that said the world was there
to be enjoyed, and what were they waiting for?

Suddenly she found herself thinking of wine
goblets filled to the brim, of golden plates piled
high with the fruits of the earth, hot suns, lovers' meetings, passion, satiation; all the good
things, the complete, perfect, richly coloured,
overflowing things that spoke of abundance
and fulfilment.

No, not spoke. Sang. As she was singing
now.

For pity's sake! she thought in alarm. Pull yourself together.

With an effort she got down to some work. There was glossy literature distributed everywhere, and she scanned it quickly, absorbing everything with her retentive memory until she felt confident of being able to do what was expected of her. Then she plunged into the crowd, at her sparkling best.

After half an hour she took a short breather. Looking around for some refreshment she found a glass of champagne put into her hand by a lean young man with very blond looks and a kind face.

'You look as if you need it, my darling,' he said, a tad theatrically.

'I do, I do,' she said thankfully. 'Bless you, Erik.'

He was an under manager at Elroys. They had been to the theatre together a few times and once she had taken him to meet her parents. Their relationship was as much friendly as romantic, but she knew that in the hotel they were considered an item.

'Back to work,' she said, finishing the champagne. 'There's a mountain to climb yet.'

She returned to the fray for more smiling
and shaking hands, until after an hour she felt
ready for another breather, and edged to the
side of the room.

'It gets to you, doesn't it?' said a voice beside her. She looked up to find the 'life-guard'
grinning down at her. They laughed together,
and it was as though she had been laughing
with this charmer all her life.

'You escaped alive, then?' she said.

'At last. He's a dear old boy but he says
everything ten times. My face muscles are frozen at ''smile''.'

Close up he was even more overwhelming,
towering over her like a friendly giant. Helen
was suddenly glad that she looked her best tonight. She knew what the dark red dress could
do for her, and if his admiring gaze was anything to go by it was doing it very nicely,
thank you!

He gave a hunted glance over his shoulder
and took her elbow. 'Let's get engaged in deep
conversation before anyone else collars me.'

They drifted into one of the window bays
and stood looking down the long canyon of
Park Avenue, far below, glittering with lights.

'Wow!' he said softly.

'Yes, it's incredible, isn't it?' she said. 'Is this your first trip to New York?' She couldn't quite place his accent beyond the fact that he wasn't American.

'It's my first trip to the States,' he said. 'I've only been here two days and I'm over-whelmed.'

'Sit down,' Helen said, 'and I'll get you something to eat.' She scooped up a collection of savouries from a table, refilled his glass, and settled thankfully on a sofa beside him.

'That sigh told volumes,' he said with a smile.

'I didn't sigh, did I?'

'Like a woman who hadn't sat down for a month. Have you been walking the streets? *No!* I didn't mean it like that.' He struck his forehead in horror, while Helen went into gales of laughter.

'That's what you say for ladies of easy vir-tue,' he groaned. 'I didn't mean that at all, I just—*oh, God*!'

'Ladies of easy virtue don't waste time standing on street corners these days,' Helen chuckled. 'Not in New York, anyway. They have penthouses and mobiles. Some of them have social secretaries. Now I suppose you're wondering how I know that?'

He pulled himself together. 'Certainly not,' he said with an attempt at dignity. 'You're a modern young woman with a wide knowledge of social conditions. And I wish I'd died before I opened my mouth.'

She would have forgiven him much for calling her a modern young woman. But no forgiveness was necessary. He delighted her.

The next moment he delighted her even more by putting his foot in it again, eyeing her identification badge and saying, 'Besides, since you work here, you must meet all kinds of lady in the hotel—'

'Not that kind of lady,' Helen said virtuously. 'The Elroy doesn't allow them.'

This time he just covered his eyes in an attitude of despair. Helen regarded him with pleasure. He had reddened with confusion, and it made him look much younger than she guessed he was. Late twenties, she reckoned. Thirty, tops.

He uncovered his eyes, pulled himself together, and looked more closely at her badge.

Something he saw there seemed to strike him, for he glanced at her in surprise. But before he could speak she refilled his glass and brought him some more to eat, trying to cover his confusion.

'Are you going to be connected with the new Italian Restaurant?' he asked, indicated a glossy brochure.

'I don't think so. I'm just here because Mr Dacre thinks of me as Italian, and it's so unfair.'

'Why is it unfair?'

'Because it's not true. I have an Italian name, which means that my parents are Italian, but I'm not. I can't convince anybody of that—including them. I'm an American. I was born in Manhattan, I grew up in Manhattan, I've never set foot in Italy in my life. I have a career and my own apartment, but Mamma still says, ''When are you going to settle down as a good wife to a nice Italian boy?'''

'And what do you say?' he asked, fascinated.

'I say there's no such thing as a nice Italian boy. They're all like Poppa.'

'And you don't like your father?'

'I adore him,' Helen said truthfully. 'I also adore my brothers, but I'll go to the stake before I marry anyone like them. Honestly, they still think they're back in the old country. And my brothers have never *seen* the old country.'

Indignation was bringing a sparkle to her eyes which turned them into pure magic, he thought. She should get mad more often. It suited her. But he knew better than to voice such an old-fashioned compliment. He didn't want her wine poured over the shirt he'd bought only that afternoon. To draw her out he asked, 'What part of Italy is the "old country"?'

'Sicily,' she said in tones of deep exasperation. 'A land where "men are men and women know their place". Would you believe, I've actually heard my father *say* that?'

'Easily. If the men of Sicily are used to their privileges they're not going to give them up without a fight.'

'Well, I know how to fight too,' she said darkly.

'I'll bet you do. If I was brave and foolhardy I might say that you show your Sicilian ancestry every time you open your mouth.'

'*What?*'

'I mean that Latin temper of yours. Pure southern Italian.' Catching her wrathful eye on him, he added hastily, 'But since I'm a coward I won't say it.'

'Very wise!' Then she sighed and said, 'I'm sorry. I go on about it too much, and I shouldn't bend your ear. That's not what you came here for.'

'Isn't it?' he murmured. 'I'm beginning to think that's exactly what I came here for.'

Next moment a glamorous young woman detached herself from the crowd, flung an arm about his shoulders and planted a theatrical kiss on his mouth.

'Bye, sweetie,' she intoned breathily.

Helen recognised Angela Havering, a fellow trainee whom she'd never liked, she now realised. Angela bestowed a second kiss for good measure before floating off on the arm of another man.

'I didn't know you were so well acquainted with Angela,' she observed.

'Just met her this evening. Like you, really.'

'But I don't call you sweetie,' she pointed out.

'You can if you want to. Have a drink with me when this is over.'

She laughed and shook her head. 'I can't. I must be going soon. I have urgent things to do.'

'Such as?'

'Oooh—' she mused, 'really important things, like planning a slow, painful death for Lorenzo Martelli.'

There was a clatter as his glass hit the table and he struggled not to choke.

'What happened?' she asked.

'Nothing,' he said, gasping slightly. 'My glass slipped. Why do you want to kill Lorenzo Martelli?'

'Well, it's either that or marry him.'

'Is—is it?' he asked, slightly wild-eyed.

'In a few minutes I have to go and join a family party at my parents' house, to meet this Martelli character. He's a Sicilian, over here on a visit. His family and mine were friends years ago, so he can't be in New York without looking us up.'

'But why have you got to marry him?'

'Because my parents have set their hearts on it.'

'But if you haven't met him—?'

'It's crazy, isn't it? They fixed tonight up while I was in Boston, and all I heard were hints about what a fine match he was and how he was bound to be looking for a good Sicilian bride—'

'Couldn't he find one of those in Sicily?'

'That's what I said. The truth is, he's probably so fat and ugly that he has to scour the world.'

He nodded wisely. 'Bound to be. You're right to make a stand.'

'Anyway, they're welcome to him. Tonight I'll sit there good as gold saying "Yes, Poppa", and "No, Poppa", like the perfect, dutiful Italian daughter.'

'Dutiful?' he couldn't resist saying. 'You?'

'They want dutiful, so I'll give them dutiful with knobs on. I may want to kick Lorenzo Martelli's shins, but I won't do it. Not tonight, at any rate. If I have to see him a second time, I won't answer for the consequences.'

'Hey, c'mon, he's not really to blame.'

'He *is* to blame,' Helen said firmly. 'Simply by existing he darkens the earth, and I'll be doing everyone a favour by exterminating him.'

He looked nervous. 'Have you decided exactly how?'

'Well, I thought of boiling in oil, but it's probably too good for him.'

'And very unimaginative.'

'You're right,' she agreed. 'Something with scorpions and spiders would be better.'

He shuddered.

'Aren't you being a bit hasty? You might fall for him and want to marry him.'

She gave him a speaking glance. 'Death would be preferable,' she said firmly. 'Mine if necessary, but his for choice.'

'Why have you got your knife into this guy? Is being Italian really so bad?'

'Being an Italian *man* is like being the devil,' she said firmly. 'They're old-fashioned, domineering, unreliable and faithless. Especially faithless.'

'Why especially faithless? I mean, if you're going to do them down, do them down on all counts, not just one.'

'It's the chief one. Do you know what they called Italian husbands? Married bachelors.

It's expected. A faithful husband is a considered a wimp. Creeps!'

'But apart from that, you think they're OK?'
he asked wryly.

'Look, I know *exactly* what's going through
Lorenzo Martelli's head at this minute.'

'You don't,' he muttered.

'What?'

'Nothing. Nothing. Tell me what's going
through his head.'

'He'll know that there are four unmarried
daughters—Patrizia, Olivia, and Carlotta—and
me. And he'll be expecting one or all of us to
make a play for him.'

He didn't answer, but he ran a finger around
the inside of his collar.

'The Martellis are rich so he'll think he's a
god of creation,' Helen said, warming to her
theme, 'loftily waiting while we parade before
him and he takes his pick.'

'The jerk!' he said with feeling.

'Exactly. Look, I know I go on about it too
much, but it's how I psyche myself up for the
evening ahead.' She looked at her watch and
said reluctantly, 'I'm afraid I have to go now.
I'll call the desk and fix a cab.'

'I'd offer you a lift,' he said, 'But as I've only just arrived I don't have any transport. Still, maybe I can escort you to your cab.'

'That would be nice,' she said cordially. 'By the way, you haven't told me your name.'

'Why, that's right—hey I see someone I must say goodbye to. Then I'll get my things from my room. See you in a moment.'

While he was gone Helen sought out Dilys who agreed to collect her luggage and take it home. Then she looked for her boss, uneasily conscious that she'd allowed herself to become distracted from her job tonight. But Mr Dacre was beaming.

'Good work, good work,' he carolled. 'Knew I could rely on you.'

Before she could ask what he meant the young man reappeared, claiming her arm. 'Let's get out of here,' he said quickly, making a gesture of farewell at Mr Dacre, but not stopping.

He had acquired an outdoor coat and a large leather bag that bulged, although she couldn't see what it contained. As they descended to the street heads turned to watch such a handsome couple.

As they left the building Helen was struck by sudden inspiration. 'Come with me.'

'What?'

'Come home with me. Come to supper.'

He looked apprehensive. 'What are you planning?'

'We just walk in together and—you know—sort of act close.'

'And then this Martelli character will know you're not available, huh?'

'That's right. Oh, please, it won't cause you any trouble, I promise.'

He doubted it. With every word he knew he was getting in deeper, storing up trouble for the moment when Helen Angolini discovered the truth. And then there would be the devil to pay. But that would make her magnificent eyes sparkle at him, and what the hell! He was a brave man! Wasn't he?

'I'll do it,' he said. 'This guy needs taking down a peg and I'm the man to do it.'

'You're wonderful, you know that?'

'I'm crazy, that's what I am.'

The cab was waiting. As they approached it Helen noticed Erik waving to her as if he wanted to speak, so she took a couple of steps towards him.

'Are you off to the lion's den?' he asked, giving her his gentle smile.

''Fraid so.'

'I'd have offered you a lift but I'm not your parents' favourite person. I'll see you tomorrow. I want to hear all about your trip. 'Bye, honey.' He kissed her cheek and went on his way.

'Boyfriend?' her companion asked as she returned to the taxi.

'Sort of. I took him home to supper once and my parents set out to sabotage any relationship we might have. Momma told him all the most embarrassing stories about my childhood and then warned him about my Latin temper.' She chuckled. 'But Erik played her at her own game beautifully. He said his ancestors were Vikings, and if a woman got mad the man just tossed her over his shoulder and strode off to the cave. Erik's the most gentle soul alive, but Momma didn't know what to say. Still, I haven't taken him there again.'

'Just see him on the quiet, huh?'

'We go out now and then.'

When they were settled in the cab she gave the driver the address on Mulberry Street. 'That's in a part of Manhattan called Little Italy, if you can believe it,' she said, exasperated.

'I believe it.'

Almost as soon as they started moving Helen had to answer her mobile.

'Yes, Mamma, I'm on my way. I'll be there in half an hour. I'm looking forward to meeting him. No really, I'm just thrilled that he's honouring us with his presence tonight.' She hung up with a sigh, and found her companion grinning at her.

'You're a very accomplished liar,' he said.

'It's simpler to say what Mamma wants to hear,' she sighed. 'Anything else she just blanks out.'

It was only a few short miles from Park Avenue to Little Italy, but the atmosphere changed swiftly from glamour and luxury to teeming life. Despite her antagonism to her background Helen could never resist a twinge of pleasure as the familiar streets appeared. This was home, whatever else she might say.

But as they glided past the butcher's shop that had been the family business as long as she could remember she saw, with a faint inward groan, that every window in the apartment above was filled with faces. They went up for three floors. When you were the eldest unmarried daughter of an Italian family, you lived your life in a spotlight.

As they got out of the cab Helen shivered for the wind was like a knife and there was snow in the air.

Her companion paid off the driver and turned to view the fascinated spectators regarding him from above. A surge of madness swept over him. He was going to be punished for what he was about to do, but it would be worth it.

'Look,' he said, taking Helen's arm, 'they're all watching us. Let's give them something to watch.'

'How do you mean?'

'Like this,' he said, drawing her close and leaning down so that his mouth was almost touching hers.

'What are you doing?' she whispered, torn between indignation at his nerve and excitement at the way his breath fluttered against her lips.

'I'm giving you the chance to stand up for yourself,' he murmured. 'Right here, where everyone can see you.'

'You make it sound so easy.'

'It *is* easy. Either you're a modern, liberated woman, or you're a dutiful daughter who'll let herself be marched into marriage with a fat old man.'

With every word his lips flickered lightly against hers, making it hard to think clearly. He was right—maybe. It was hard to tell when little tremors of excitement were scurrying through her.

'I don't normally kiss men I've only just met,' she protested.

'Well, they don't know we've only just met.'

'But I don't even know your na—'

The gentle pressure of his lips cut off the last word, and she felt his arms tighten about her just a little, not enough to be threatening, just enough to say he meant business. He was laughing too, inviting her to share the joke even while he kissed her with lips she instinctively sensed had kissed a thousand times before.

Those lips knew far too much, she thought. They were experts in teasing a woman until her head was in a whirl. And they brought back the visions that had assailed her when she first saw him, visions of abundance, riches and sunshine. The wind was as cold as ever, but now she was filled with warmth, melting her, overwhelming her.

'It would look more convincing if you kissed me back,' he murmured. 'Put your arms around my neck.'

Her mind told him to stop his nonsense, but her hands were already sliding up until she could touch his hair, wind her fingers in it, relish the soft, springiness against her palm. She was pulling him closer because she wanted more of him, longed for what only the firm warmth of his mouth could give her. And when she found herself kissing him fervently back it was useless to pretend that she was only trying to 'make it convincing'. She was doing this because she wanted to.

She flattened her hands against his chest. 'I think we've done enough,' she said in a shaking voice.

'We haven't even started,' he whispered, and even then she noticed that his voice too was shaking. Looking up she saw his eyes in the near darkness, and thought there was a look of astonishment.

'Let me go,' she said urgently. She was suddenly full of alarm. She *had* to be free of him before it was too late. Trying to strike a lighter note she said, 'If Lorenzo Martelli saw that he might take a stiletto to you.'

'Let him come. I'm brave enough for anything tonight.'

There was the sound of doors, voices raised in excitement. Suddenly he grasped Helen's hand. 'You will take my side in the row, won't you?' he begged.

'There may not be a row.'

'Oh, yes,' he said in a voice that was hollow with approaching doom. 'There's going to be a row.'

She stared at him, puzzled. But before she could ask, her mother was on them, and incredibly she was laughing, hugging her eldest daughter to her and muttering, 'What a clever girl you are!'

'Mamma, I have someone with me. Didn't you see what we were—?'

'Oh course I saw. We all did. When Poppa told me who he was we got out the best champagne.'

'Poppa knows him?'

'He collected him from the airport two days ago. There now! Didn't we choose a splendid husband for you?'

She was suddenly dizzy. There was a fog about her head, but not thick enough to shield her from the incredible, the monstrous, the outrageous truth. There was Poppa pumping the young man by the hand, bellowing, *'Lorenzo!'* There were her sisters, surrounding him excitedly, urging him inside.

And there was Lorenzo Martelli, letting himself be hauled away, meeting Helen's stormy eyes from the safety of a distance, and giving her a shrug in which guilt, helplessness and mischief were equally mixed, before turning tail and seeking refuge in the safety of the house.

CHAPTER TWO

MAMMA was almost bouncing up and down in her excitement, kissing her daughter again and again.

'Isn't that wonderful?' she enthused. 'Fancy the two of you liking each other at once! Just wait until your Aunt Lucia in Maryland hears about this.'

Helen blanched at the thought of this story spreading all over Maryland. How long before it got to California? 'Mamma, don't tell Aunt Lucia anything just now.'

'You're right. Wait until you've got his ring on your finger.'

'*Mamma—*'

'OK, OK. But you gotta tell me how you met him.'

'He was at the hotel reception tonight.'

'Of course. He wants to sell them his vegetables. Oh, it'll be a marriage made in heaven.'

'It isn't a marriage made anywhere,' Helen said crossly. 'I'm not marrying him.'

Signora Angolini screamed. 'What you mean? What kind of a girl kisses a man in front of the whole street and then says she won't marry him?'

'It's not in front of the—' A prickle on her spine caused her to look up the high buildings. Row upon row they rose, and wherever she looked the windows were packed with smiling faces.

'I think we'd better get indoors,' she said faintly. One ghastly fact was becoming clearer by the moment. There was no way she could tell her family the truth. If kissing her 'fiancé' in the street was bad, kissing a man whose identity she hadn't known was a hundred times worse. The Angolini family would never recover from the shame.

Their home was an apartment over the butcher's shop that was Nicolo Angolini's pride and joy. Although large, it was always slightly cramped by two parents and three daughters. Tonight it was packed to the seams with the three sons, their wives and children. By the time Helen and Mamma had climbed the stairs the introductions had been made, and Lorenzo was the centre of a smiling crowd.

Now Helen discovered the purpose of the leather bag. Lorenzo had come bearing gifts, wine and delicacies from Sicily that made Mamma tearful as she recalled the homeland that she had last seen as a girl. Helen was so touched by her mother's happiness that she almost forgave Lorenzo. Almost.

Her sisters were in ecstasies.

'He's really handsome,' Patrizia whispered, seconded by Olivia and Carlotta. 'Oh, Elena, you're so lucky.'

'My name is Helen, and one more word out of any of you will be your last,' she muttered.

'But I want to be a bridesmaid,' wailed Carlotta, who was fifteen.

'You'll be a statistic in the missing persons' column in a minute,' Helen warned.

Her sisters exchanged significant looks, understanding that Elena (who had always been 'difficult') might be a little sensitive just now.

Turning away from them she edged her way up to Lorenzo, until she got close enough to mutter. 'We have to talk.'

'Look, I'm sorry—'

'You're going to be.'

'It just happened.'

To the delight of her whole family she put her hands on his shoulders, gazing up into his face with an utterly charming smile. 'You're a scheming rat,' she murmured.

'I didn't mean it to be like it was.'

'Have you told my family the truth?'

'No.'

'Good. Because if you do, you're dead.' She glided away, still smiling. Lorenzo gulped.

The folding doors between the two main rooms had been pushed back, creating one large room, connected to the kitchen by a hatch, through which Mamma passed enough food to supply an army. Pride of place was given to a variety of meat courses.

Everyone wanted to talk to Lorenzo, which saved Helen from having to do so. She needed time to compose her thoughts. Memories of the things she'd said tonight flitted through her horrified brain. She'd actually told him that her parents were trying to arrange their marriage. And he not only hadn't warned her, but he'd joined in her vilification of Lorenzo Martelli.

To cap his iniquity he'd tricked her into accepting his kiss, and actually kissing him back. At this point her thoughts became lost in disorder. Warmth rose in her and she had a horrible feeling that it was showing in her cheeks.

Great! Now he would see her blushing, and that would make him even more full of himself. She looked at him angrily across the table, and found that he was watching her, as she'd feared. But not as though he were pleased with himself. There was a question in his eyes, and his lips wore a half smile that she would have found delightful under other circumstances.

It was all part of the trickery, she warned herself. Having insulted her, he was now bent on winning forgiveness on easy terms. Well, he could think again!

Lorenzo was talking about his family back in Palermo. Helen gathered that his father had died some years earlier, but his mother was still alive, although in frail health.

'She called me last week,' Mamma said, 'to say you were coming. And I told her you would always be welcome in our home.'

'Well, you've certainly made me welcome tonight,' Lorenzo assured her with his charming smile that took in everyone at the table.

'Do you have any brothers and sisters?' Carlotta wanted to know.

'Two brothers, Renato and Bernardo, both older than me. No sisters, but a sister-in-law. Renato has recently married an English woman called Heather, and their first baby is due later this year.'

Poppa was frowning. 'I didn't know your parents had three sons,' he said. 'I thought it was only two.'

'No, there are three of us.' Lorenzo's smile was still perfect, but Helen detected a fleeting tension in him, and noticed how adroitly he turned the conversation.

He was wonderful in company, Helen realised. He could be 'man-to-man' with her father and brothers, while charming Mamma and making her sisters laugh. In no time at all he had them all on his side, which struck Helen as a really dirty trick.

The most difficult part of the evening was that for once she had her parents' total, un-qualified approval. They had picked out a suit-able husband, and instead of arguing she had moved to first base in a couple of hours. In this atmosphere it was impossible to tell them that their choice was a devious, unscrupulous deceiver who ought to be hung up by his thumbs until he promised never to approach a woman again.

Lorenzo, watching her, read her thoughts with tolerable accuracy, but he was too much occupied with getting his bearings to worry about the retribution awaiting him. As a Sicilian he was used to large gatherings, but it was taking all his presence of mind to hold his own in this one. Apart from brothers and sisters and aunts and uncles, there were also a couple of Mamma's nieces with their husbands. Of these, the one who stuck in Lorenzo's mind was Giorgio, because he disliked him so much.

Giorgio was a huge man with a spiteful face and a bullying nature. He was also blatantly on the make, and lost no time in telling Lorenzo about his family back in Sicily who'd been trying to sell their produce to Martellis for years, but had been scandalously rejected. He implied that now he expected this injustice to be put right.

Lorenzo fenced with him and escaped as soon as he could, giving a huge sigh of relief.

That was one more reason to be glad he wasn't marrying Helen Angolini. Even if she hadn't rejected him first.

To be fair, he was beginning to understand her feelings. The men of the Angolini family were of a type that was becoming outdated even in Sicily where tradition still prevailed. In this household male superiority was still taken as the norm. Only the younger women, who spent their working lives outside in a different world, questioned it. The men, enclosed in the haven of Little Italy, thought nothing had changed.

The dinner was superb and Lorenzo was able to praise his hostess's cooking with real pleasure. She smiled and accepted his tribute with a few words, but when her husband intervened to say that Angolini meats were second to none she retired and let him take the credit.

Lorenzo tried again, but this time it was Giorgio who butted in, interrupting Signora Angolini in a way that nobody would have been allowed to do with his own mother. Mamma's reaction was to rise with a smile and a nod to her daughters to help her clear away.

After that the party broke into two groups, women washing up and making coffee, and men gathering to talk.

The evening culminated in a grand family toast to Lorenzo, and an invitation to supper whenever he wished. At last the family began to drift off to their own homes, in some cases just across the street. The party was over. Poppa yawned. He had to get up early next morning.

'Time for me to go,' Lorenzo said heartily.

'No, no, you stay a while,' Mamma protested. 'We're all going to bed, but Elena can make you some more coffee.'

'Yes, do stay,' Helen said affably, but with her hand implacably through Lorenzo's arm. 'We have a lot to talk about.'

He gave her a hunted look.

The younger girls drifted off to bed. Mamma and Poppa beamed and departed. Helen surveyed her prey.

'*You* are Lorenzo Martelli,' she said through gritted teeth.

'Yes,' he admitted.

'And you've been Lorenzo Martelli all this time?'

'Well, it's not something that comes and goes,' he said defensively. 'I'm kinda stuck with it.'

'You were Lorenzo Martelli while we were talking at the hotel?'

'As far as I know.'

'And you were Lorenzo Martelli when you kissed me?'

'Guilty!'

'Even though you knew I disliked you?'

'You disliked some guy who doesn't exist,' he protested. 'That wasn't me.'

'It sure was. I disliked Lorenzo Martelli then and I dislike him ten times more now that I know he's a devious scoundrel without a shred of honour. Shall I tell you what I'd like to do to you?'

'I think I'd rather you didn't.'

'Kissing me like that was a dishonourable act, and if I told Poppa the full truth you'd be mincemeat.'

'Not if he wants you to marry me,' he was unwise enough to say. *'All right, all right!'* He backed off fast. 'Whatever you were going to do, don't do it. I shouldn't have stolen that kiss, and I'm sorry, but I got carried away by your beauty and—'

'I'm warning you, Martelli, don't insult my intelligence. You should be ashamed of yourself. No *gentleman* would do what you did.'

'I'm not a gentleman,' he protested quickly, evidently seeing this as some sort of defence. 'I never pretended to be one.'

'You got that kiss from me by false pretences.'

'You're right. How about I give it back?'

'Come one step closer and you're dead.'

'Aw, now look, that kiss wasn't a one-sided business. You kissed me back.'

'It's a lie! Nothing on earth would persuade me to kiss that man.'

'Will you quit talking about me as though I wasn't here? And don't tell me I don't know when a woman's kissing me.'

'That will be your experience talking, I suppose?' she asked, her eyes kindling. 'Your *vast* experience?

He took a nervous step behind a chair. 'Fair to middling,' he said self-consciously.

'Hah!'

He rallied his forces, such as they were. 'May I ask what you mean by "Hah!" in that voice?'

'Never you mind.'

'You don't know what you mean by it, do you? When a woman knows she's talking nonsense she says "Hah!"'

'Oh, really? Well, consider this. Everyone in the street saw us kissing, and that makes it a very public thing. I can't tell them I didn't know your name because that would bring shame and disgrace on my parents, my brothers, my sisters, my nephews and nieces, my aunts and uncles, *their* aunts and uncles, their ancestors, their cousins and the whole shooting match going right back to Sicily. What's more, my mother is dying to tell Aunt Lucia in Maryland, who will certainly pass it on to Aunt Zita in Idaho, who will telegraph it to Los Angeles. This is a Sicilian family. Today Manhattan. Tomorrow the world. Do you realise,' she demanded, incensed, 'that now they'll *expect* me to marry you?'

'No problem. I can take care of that.'

'How?'

'I swear I'll never propose. My solemn word, so you're quite safe. And to make doubly sure, I'll talk to your parents and tell them I've decided I don't like you very much.'

'After what they saw in the street?'

'I'll tell them you're a lousy kisser—*don't throw that*!'

He ducked as a book came flying past his head and struck the wall with a loud crack.

'Out,' she told him.

'Shouldn't we fix our next date? They'll expect it—'

'*Out!*'

He got as far as the door before saying, 'Are you spending the night here?'

'No, I'm going back to my apartment.'

'Then shouldn't we be leaving together?'

Helen breathed hard. 'Signor Martelli, if you'd been listening to a word I said, you'd know that I would prefer not to share the same *planet* with you, never mind the same cab.'

'I know,' he said gravely. 'I'm not keen on you either, but we have to make these sacrifices.'

'Who'll know if we leave together or not?'

'Anyone who's standing at their window.'

The appalling truth of this hit her like a sledge-hammer. 'Which means the whole street,' she groaned. 'I'll call us a cab.'

When she'd finished making the call he was holding up her coat, and Helen put her arms in the sleeves, accepting the inevitable. They had to leave together, or there would be talk, and there'd already been too much of that.

Luckily the cab appeared quickly and they both behaved with perfect propriety. Lorenzo gave her his arm down the steps of the building, which were slippery from frost. She allowed him to show her to the vehicle and open the door for her. She never looked up but she was burningly conscious of many pairs of eyes watching from above.

As the car's tail lights disappeared around the corner Mamma Angolini dropped the curtain of her bedroom window, and heaved a sentimental sigh. 'Did you see the way he handed her in?'

Poppa, standing beside her, frowned, 'But what were those noises earlier?'

'Oh, that's nothing,' she told him cheerfully. 'They were just having a lovers' tiff.'

*   *   *

In the back of the cab Lorenzo said placatingly, 'Why don't we stop for a drink somewhere, and straighten this out?'

'There's nothing to straighten out,' she said coolly. 'I'll drop you off at the Elroy and go on alone.'

'I see,' he said glumly. 'The frozen mitt treatment.'

'You're lucky it's not the frozen sock-on-the-jaw treatment.'

She should have known better. He stuck out his chin, pointing to it hopefully.

'Oh, stop it,' she said, trying not to smile. He was wicked and irresistible.

'No, go on, thump me if it'll make you feel better.'

She abandoned the struggle not to laugh, clenched her fist and punched his chin very, very gently. Another mistake. He seized her hand and kissed it.

The swift action took her by surprise, invading her senses before she could suppress the memory of that other kiss, full on the lips, by a young man who kissed subtly and with intent. It all came back to her now, so that although his lips were moving across her hand she seemed to feel them on her mouth. She must tell him now, coolly and primly, that this must stop at once.

But she felt neither cool nor prim. She felt as though waves of warmth were laving her, and thoughts of wine and roses were going through her head.

Just when she was starting to panic, he stopped, releasing her hand suddenly and abandoning her to a sense of loss that sent warnings jolting through her. *Basta!* Enough!

'There's Elroys,' she said, with relief. 'Don't worry about my parents. I'll call them tomorrow and explain that you and I won't be seeing each other in future.'

'But what about our wedding?' he asked, sounding hurt.

'I shall tell Momma that we decided against it.'

'After what she saw?'

'We got carried away. On reflection we realised we were mistaken.'

In the semi darkness of the cab she could see his teeth gleam. 'About what?'

'About—about being carried away.'

'I don't mind if you want to carry me away. We could—'

'Now you cut it out,' she flashed. 'That innocent little boy charm may floor my mother but it leaves me cold.'

'I was afraid it did,' he said mournfully.

The cab drew to a halt. 'Goodnight, Mr Martelli. It was a pleasure meeting you and I wish you every success.'

'No, you don't. You wish you could boil me in oil.'

'I was giving you the polite version.'

'In that case, thank you, Miss Angolini, for a lovely evening. I hope our paths cross again one day.'

She returned his smile with deadly intent. 'Not if I can prevent it,' she said. 'Goodnight. Sleep well.'

She watched him go into the hotel and vanish from sight. That was that. Somehow she would contrive not to see him again.

She gave the driver the address of the apartment on East 77th Street that she shared with Dilys.

Her friend was home ahead of her, dressed for bed. 'So how was your evening?' she asked. 'I saw you talking to the life-guard. Any good?'

''Fraid not,' Helen said, yawning. 'Handsome on the outside, but nothing to him. Boring really.'

Next morning Helen found a message to report to Jack Dacre.

'I've got a new assignment for you,' he said, 'and seeing as how you and Signor Martelli have already broken the ice, I know you'll enjoy it.'

'Really?' Helen was holding herself in neutral.

'I want you to look after him. Apparently his English isn't as good as I first thought. He admits that a lot of the time he's only pretending to understand. He's happier in Sicilian dialect, which I gather you speak, so you can act as his interpreter. That way you can keep an eye on his other dealings. It all works out very well.'

'Especially for Lorenzo Martelli,' Helen murmured wrathfully as she knocked on Lorenzo's door.

It opened apparently of its own accord. She walked in and found him tucked behind the door, regarding her with apprehension.

'Will you stop playing the fool?' she said, half laughing, half exasperated.

'It's nice to see you.'

'You're just up to your tricks again. Pretending your English is no good, when I know it's perfect.'

'Is true, is true,' he clowned in excruciating stage Italian. 'Me no spikka da English.'

She just looked at him, trying not to smile, but it was hard to be severe when the dancing light in his eyes was tempting her to dreams of delight.

'I've been detailed to assist you,' she said, trying to sound business like. 'Shall we discuss the programme for the day?'

'Why don't you show me the sights?'

'Mr Martelli, I'm a busy woman.'

'OK, OK,' he said in resignation. 'It was worth a try. Here's a list of places I have to visit. There are no other hotels in New York, but several restaurants.'

'None of these are Italian restaurants,' she objected, studying the list.

'Of course. That's the idea. I'm out to make converts and Italians already know that Martelli produce is the best.'

'I shouldn't have asked.'

'True. As a good Sicilian, you should have known.'

'Lorenzo—'

'I didn't mean it, I didn't mean it. Let's go.'

Over the next few hours she began to give him a grudging respect. Lorenzo was a first-class salesman who used his charm to get himself into the customer's good graces before knocking him for six with the quality of his product. By the evening he had a solid wad of orders, all of which he'd promised to fulfil by the next day, having taken the precaution of hiring a warehouse and filling it in readiness.

'And I'm exhausted,' he complained at last. 'Let's go in here and relax.'

The place he'd chosen at random was called Fives, and it overlooked the Hudson. Darkness had fallen and lights glittered along the river, entrancing Helen, even though she was used to such views. Tonight all her senses seemed heightened. Even edge was a little clearer, each colour a little sharper.

She felt good. It had been a pleasant day with a delightful companion, for when Lorenzo wasn't being maddening he was amusing. Recently her life had been all hard work and not enough laughter, she realised.

'I feel as though I'd done a week's work in one day,' he observed.

'So do I.'

'I shouldn't have made you work so hard, should I?'

'Right. I was only supposed to be translating for you.'

'But I don't need a translator,' he said innocently.

'No, but you sure needed a dogsbody—make a note of this, jot that down—'

He blew a kiss at her. 'You take the best notes in the business. Let's get them into the computer while they're still fresh.' He produced his laptop and studied some scraps of paper. 'I can't read your writing.'

'I'll put them into the computer. You get me something to eat before I faint with hunger.'

The waiter arrived with the menu. Lorenzo ordered drinks, and when they were alone he made an excited exclamation.

'This is a vegetarian restaurant. Just what I need. We'll try as many dishes as possible to see where we can improve them.' He began to read from the menu, pausing at each dish to observe, 'I'll bet I can improve on that.'

The drinks arrived, and between taking sips and tapping into the laptop Helen failed to notice that the waiter had returned, taken an order from Lorenzo, and departed.

'But I didn't tell you what I wanted,' she protested.

He looked awkward. 'The things is, I thought we should cover as wide a range as possible between us so—'

'So you ordered for me something that suited you?'

'Well—yes.'

'That's the sort of thing my father would do,' she said wrathfully.

'Ah, but that's different. Your father is simply an old-fashioned patriarch. I act from nobler motives.'

'Such as?'

'I'm making money.'

It was no use trying to out-talk him. She sighed, but her lips were twitching.

'Talking about your father,' he said, as their starters arrived, 'I begin to understand what you mean. He's very traditional, to put it mildly.'

Helen nodded. 'In some ways Papa is a wonderful man. He's kind, and he works long, long hours for his family. But in return he expects to make all the big decisions. Mamma simply has no say.' Her mischievous spirit made her add, 'A bit like you just now.'

'No,' he said seriously. 'I was nine years old when my father died, but I remember him well, and I'm sure he never spoke to his wife as brusquely as your father does. I'm also sure I'll never speak to mine like that.'

She pointed a courgette at him. 'I'm not marrying you, Martelli.'

He grinned. 'Tell your father that. He was practically planning the wedding present last night.'

'You tell him. You're the man, the authority, the one who speaks while the little woman is silent.'

'Who, me?' He looked alarmed.

'Yes, you. Are you a man or a mouse?'

'A mouse,' he said promptly. 'It's much safer that way.'

'You mean you don't have to explain to my father,' she chuckled.

He regarded her askance. 'You're so contrary you'd refuse to marry me just to annoy him.'

'That and plenty of other reasons,' she assured him.

He made a parade of relief. 'Phew! Then I'm safe!'

'Eat your starter,' she advised him. 'The next course will be here soon and I can't wait to find out what The Great Man ordered on my behalf.'

CHAPTER THREE

THE next dish was bean and artichoke salad, which was delicious. As Lorenzo poured her a glass of light wine he asked, 'What about your sisters? Do they feel the same as you about your father and all the rest?'

'No,' she said, realising the truth of the words as she said them. 'Oh, they have arguments with Mamma and Poppa, but they're only normal growing-up stuff. They don't feel suffocated by the whole family thing as I do.'

'You feel suffocated by your family?' he asked with a frown.

'By their expectations. Last night, when they saw us together in the street, nobody was surprised. They thought it was just the plan working out.'

'But you're going to trump them with Erik?'

'It's not about Erik—it's not about any man. Why should everyone think that if I'm not romancing one man I must be romancing another?'

'Because romance is natural,' he protested.
'Men and women pair off. That's how the human race gets re-stocked.'

'But can't there be more to life? Suppose I
see myself as an hotel manager rather than a
''re-stocking agent''?'

'Can't you be both?'

'Not if I marry a Sicilian,' she said firmly.

'I see,' he said thoughtfully, 'so if I were to
go down on one knee and say, ''Be mine forever'', I could count on you saying no?'

'You could count on me having you placed
under restraint. After what you know about
me, you'd have to be losing your wits to want
me.'

'That's very true. Thanks for the warning.'

They smiled together and she said, 'If you
knew how nice it is to be able to talk freely,
knowing I'm not going to get cries of horror.'

'That's what friends are for.' He gave her a
sudden intense look. 'I think you need a
friend.'

'Men and women can't be friends,' she said
mechanically.

'Who said that? Not you.'

'No, Mamma. And Poppa. At different times. Poppa says it's impossible because women just don't understand anything outside the kitchen. And Mamma says it's impossible because men only want "one thing".'

'Well, we're going to prove them wrong,' he said gently. 'Men and women *need* to be friends because we each light up the other side of the world for the other.'

'That's what I think too,' she said eagerly. 'But from where I come from—'

'And where *I* come from,' Lorenzo agreed. 'But they're wrong. It can be done.'

He stretched out his hand and she took it, smiling. Out of the corner of his eye Lorenzo noticed people grinning at them. Helen looked around and understood.

'You know what they're thinking?' she said.

'Yes, they think we're in love. Why else should a man and woman clasp hands and smile into each other's eyes?'

For a tense moment they both fell silent. Why else?

'If we told them the truth they wouldn't believe it,' she said.

'Right. How could they understand that we've discovered the second most important relationship of our lives?'

'Second?'

'I suppose one day I'll fall in love for good. And you'll meet a man you don't reject in the first five minutes.' He squeezed her hand lightly to show he was joking. 'And they'll mean more to each of us than we mean to each other.'

'Yes, I suppose they will,' she said blankly.

'But until then—?'

'Friendship comes first.' Then something occurred to her. 'What did you mean, ''fall in love for good?'' How do you usually fall in love?'

'Well—you know.' He coloured.

'Come on,' she laughed. 'Tell your friend. You're ''faithless and unreliable'' aren't you?'

'They invented the words just for me,' he admitted. 'You were very clever to see through me so fast. Now, where's our food?'

While they were waiting for the next course Helen asked, 'Why were you suddenly on edge last night when Poppa asked about your brothers? Do you have one or two?'

'I have one full brother and one half brother.'

'You mean, one of your parents was married before?'

'Not exactly,' he said uneasily. 'I know you're going to think the worst of this, but my father had another relationship with a lady called Marta. And Bernardo is Marta's son.'

'Another relationship? While he was married to your mother?'

'Yes.'

'And your mother knows?'

'She always knew. She promised Poppa that if he died she would take care of his other family.'

'His other—? Well, of all the—' Helen was rendered speechless, giving Lorenzo a chance to enjoy the flames that glowed in her eyes. 'Are you telling me that she did that?' she demanded when she'd recovered her voice. 'She actually befriended the other woman when your father died?'

'She didn't have to. My father and Marta died together. But Mamma brought Bernardo into our home to be raised like her own sons.'

Helen stared at him in horrified disbelief. 'Your mother must be a saint,' she said at last.

'She is.'

'She actually—? I don't believe this. That poor woman.'

'Mamma isn't a poor woman,' Lorenzo said firmly. 'She rules us all with a rod of iron.'

'But her heart must have been broken.'

'I don't think it was. She and my father always got on well.'

'You mean, she put up with whatever he did because she had no choice, and made the best of it. Well, you know what I think about that.'

'Yes, but that wasn't why I didn't mention it last night. Surrounded by your family, and your sisters being so young—'

It dawned on Helen that Lorenzo was embarrassed. She smiled, liking him again.

'You're really straight out of the old country after all, aren't you?' she asked.

'Well, I am a Sicilian,' he admitted. 'But then, so are you.'

'No way.'

'Deny it all you like, you can't escape it.'

'You're asking for this sauce in your lap, Martelli.'

'OK, I give in.'

'Tell me some more about your half brother. Is he really a member of the family?'

'He could be if he wanted. If anything, he rejects us, not the other way around. He won't call himself Martelli. He sticks to Tornese because it was his mother's name. We don't see much of Bernardo. He lives in a little mountain village called Montedoro, where he was born. He despises money, won't even take his rightful share of the inheritance. Recently he fell in love with an English woman, Angie. Everything was fine and we were waiting for the announcement when he suddenly found out that she was rich. That was it. He sent her away.'

'And she let him?'

'Not her. Angie's a doctor, so she bought up the practise in Montedoro, and now she's living just down the street from him. He's mad as fire, but he can't budge her. She won't stand for that nonsense about knowing her place any more than you do.'

'Good for her. I like the sound of Angie.'

'You'd like her if you met her. And I think she's going to win. She's blonde and fluffy, and looks as if a wind would blow her over, but she's got more guts than anyone I've ever known.'

'How did they meet? Was she visiting Sicily or was he travelling?'

'She came to Sicily with Heather,' Lorenzo said vaguely, and again Helen had the feeling that he was embarrassed about something.

'Heather's married to your older brother, Renato, right?

'Right.' Before she could ask any more questions he added quickly, 'This is good food but I could make it better. We have a potential customer.'

He continued on this subject throughout the next course. He was full of ideas, and Helen had to admit that he was an excellent businessman.

'I saw Giorgio bending your ear last night,' she said when he paused for breath. 'I needn't ask what about.'

'Why aren't we selling his family's goods?' Lorenzo confirmed. 'I've already been in touch with Renato about them. Their goods are borderline. They've been told to improve the quality and try again, but instead of doing something they just wail about the injustice.

'There's no excuse for poor produce,' he went on. 'Sicily is the most fertile land in the world. Everything grows there, and grows well if it's properly tended.'

Something seemed to come over him as he began to talk about his country. He spoke in a new way, with a feeling she could only call love. This light playboy with his silk shirts and easy manners had a passionate attachment to the land that breathed through every word. She watched him, fascinated, and at last he noticed, and smiled.

'The Martellis have to know about the land,' he said. 'It's how we earn our bread.'

'It's more than knowing about it,' she said gently.

'Well—yes. It's part of me and I'm part of it. I can't help it. I go away but I always go back, and I always will. It's part of being Sicilian. You never quite escape.'

She smiled sympathetically, but inwardly she was thinking how right she'd been to reject him at the start. Lorenzo was a man who would always win love easily. His charm, his looks, his kind heart, were made to be loved, and a woman would have to be armoured in advance—as she was—to avoid the danger.

'How long will you be in New York?' she asked.

'A few more days. Then I move on to Boston, Philadelphia, Detroit, Chicago and Pittsburgh. That's as much as I can do in one trip. At least, it's as much as Renato will let me do. Then he'll want a full report to see if I'm achieving all he expects and, if I am, he'll let me come back here.'

'He sounds like a slave driver.'

'He does his best. Since our father died Renato has got a bit patriarchal, and I try to assert myself to escape from under his thumb. When I get back to my room tonight I shall have to call him with full details.'

At the end of the meal he asked to speak to the chef. The talk then became entirely businesslike, with Helen taking notes until her head whirled.

'Renato should be proud of you,' she said when they were out on the pavement. 'What now? Do you want to sample some New York nightlife?'

'What time is it? *Nine o'clock?* It's the early hours in Palermo. Renato will kill me.' He hailed a cab and kissed her cheek as it drew up. 'I can't thank you enough for your help. I won't trouble you again tomorrow, but perhaps we could have a drink before I leave?'

'That would be delightful,' she said, in a daze.

'I'll call you. 'Bye.'

She saw him once, briefly, before he went to Boston. After Philadelphia he returned to New York for one night and dutifully accompanied her to supper at home, where he played the bashful suitor in a way that made it hard for Helen to keep a straight face, but which also fended off awkward questions.

Then he was off again. During the next two months he kept in touch only fitfully which, Helen told herself, was a relief, as her training period was coming to and end and she was snowed under with work.

She was doing a stint with Erik now, and learning a lot for he was an excellent teacher.

'I shall never get the hang of these statistics,' she said at the end of one long afternoon. 'This column seems very odd.'

He came and leaned over her to see where she pointed.

'The figures look poor but it's an illusion,' he said. 'We've had to artificially exclude some revenue but—'

He went on explaining for a few minutes, and she glanced up with a grateful smile. 'You explain it so well. Thank you.'

He looked pleased. 'I expect you're ready for an end of the day drink.'

'Yes, please.'

Neither of them noticed the door opening, or the young man who stood on the threshold, stiffening at the sight of their smiling closeness.

'Hello,' Lorenzo said.

Erik went to shake Lorenzo's hand. 'Good to see you back,' he said. 'Everyone is extremely pleased with Martelli produce.'

'That's what I wanted to hear,' Lorenzo said at once. 'I couldn't resist dropping in before I return home, just to see how it's faring in your restaurant.'

'We were going to go for a drink,' Erik said easily. 'Why don't you dump your things in your room then come down and join us in the Empire Bar?'

'Great. I'll be right down.'

But when he returned a few minutes later he found Helen sitting in the bar alone.

'Erik was called away,' she said. 'He says I'm to entertain you.'

She spoke coolly. It was two weeks since his last email, and then he just walked in as though he owned the place.

'We eat in the restaurant here,' she went on, 'so that the chef can discuss your produce and how he wants to increase his orders.'

'Oh, do we? Get your coat.'

'What?'

'We're going somewhere else. I want to talk to you not the chef.'

'But your orders—'

'They can wait until tomorrow.'

They found a small bar near the river. Spring was here and it was still light enough to see the water and the surrounding life. Helen realised how much she had missed him. With Lorenzo away there was nobody to talk too, and he would be leaving again so soon.

'How have you been?' he asked. 'Are your parents giving you grief?'

'A bit, but I had a stroke of luck. I took Mamma on a shopping trip, and we finished with tea at Elroys, and Erik came and joined us. She'd met him before and she knew I'd been seeing him, so when he'd gone she got very cross on your behalf and asked what I was playing at. I told her I couldn't decide between the two of you. That made her really mad. She demanded how could I behave so badly to "that nice boy", as she insisted on calling you.'

He grinned. 'You didn't disillusion her, did you?'

'Nothing would disillusion her. Telling her what you're really like would be a waste of time.'

'So when you announce your engagement to Erik she'll be partly prepared for it?'

'If I ever do.'

'Well, the two of you made a very cosy picture together when I walked in.'

'He was explaining something to me.'

'Sure, sure. I should congratulate you on getting him where you want him.'

'How do you mean?'

'C'mon, Helen. A guy doesn't leave his special lady alone with another guy unless he feels pretty safe.'

'Well, maybe he doesn't think of you as another guy,' she said nettled. 'He knows what good friends we are—'

'Just good friends,' Lorenzo muttered.

'What?'

'Nothing, nothing.' He looked at her sharply. 'You look tired. What is it? Is life giving you a hard time?'

'No, I'm just snowed under with working for my exams.'

'What exams?'

'Elroys has its own exam system. The people who come out top get the best jobs. I've simply got to be one of them.'

Her vehemence made him look at her sharply. 'Hey, steady on,' he said. 'Helen, don't take everything so seriously. You'll wear yourself out. Ease up.'

'But I can't ease up. It means so much—my whole life—and it all turns on doing well now. I told you—'

'Yes, you told me, about your family and needing to escape, but let me tell you something. Sometimes escape doesn't lie in the direction you think.'

'I don't know where it lies. It's a bit like being caught in a maze and you don't know the way out, but you know there is one.'

'And sometimes it was right behind you all the time, and you overlooked it because it was so obvious.'

She eyed him suspiciously. 'What does that mean?'

'It's not a proposal, so stop bristling.'

'I'm sorry. Am I that bad?'

'Yes,' he said gently. 'You are that bad. You need looking after.' He gave her an intent look. 'And you can't tell them at home, can you? Because they'd try to use it as a weapon to make you give up.'

She nodded. 'That's exactly how it is. You're the first person who's understood that. It's lonely.'

'But you don't have to be lonely any more. We can talk. Look, tomorrow night—'

'I have to stay in tomorrow night. Dilys will be out so I can work in peace. I'm sorry.'

'Don't be sorry, we'll still be seeing each other.'

'But I've told you—'

'I'm going to cook your supper, like a good friend. Then I'll clear the table and melt into the background while you work. At various intervals I'll bring you coffee, then melt again.'

She looked up at him and spoke with wicked relish. 'And wash the dishes?'

He gulped. 'I'll even do the dishes.'

She only half believed that he meant it, but the following evening he was waiting, laden with bags, when she left her office. As soon as they were in her apartment, he said, 'You get on with what you want to do, while I cook.'

He brought her some coffee in the first few minutes, then started his preparations in the kitchen with the concentration of a maestro. He moved so quietly that once she looked up to make sure he was there. He smiled briefly and ordered her 'back to work at once', with a severity that made her smile.

The meal was a delicious creation of tender meats, beautifully cooked. But an incredible suspicion was overtaking Helen.

'This meat—?'

'Angolini's finest. I went to your father's shop this afternoon and asked him what you liked. He told me about this. He said when you were a little girl it was your favourite, and he'd make it for you himself sometimes.'

'Yes, he did,' she said, remembering. 'He used to say, "My best meat for my best lady." He could be lovely. I'd forgotten that.'

'I wish you could have seen his face this afternoon as he showed me how to cook it the way you like.'

'But it's years since—' She broke off.

'It may be years but he remembers every detail of what his "best lady" liked,' Lorenzo said. 'Now you get back to work. The next course is going to take a while if I'm to get it the way your mother showed me.'

Having rendered her totally speechless he retreated into the kitchen.

He served her peaches stewed in wine, with cream, washed down with the best coffee she had ever tasted.

'Did you say my mother?' she asked at last.

'Poppa sent me upstairs to get her advice, and later he joined us. I think she'd told him how you're playing me false with Erik, because he assumed I was laying myself out to win you back. He advised me against it. He said it gave a woman improper ideas about having power. Mamma told him to stop talking nonsense.'

'Mamma said that to Poppa? I don't believe it.'

'It's different when their kids aren't around, Helen. All that bossy stuff is for your benefit. When he's in her kitchen he practically stands to attention if she talks to him. And he was fetching and carrying things from cupboards when she told him to.'

She smiled, but she only half believed it.

Afterwards she tried to help him with the washing up.

'No way,' he said, fending her off. 'We agreed it was my job.'

'But I can't let you, after you cooked that lovely meal. Think of your macho image.'

'I never had a macho image,' he said sorrowfully. 'I just did what my mother told me. ''Gigi, do this; Gigi, do that.'' '

'She called you Gigi?'

'It's short for Luigi, which is my second name.'

'And you did what she told you?'

'Always,' he said, suspiciously innocent. 'I was scared of her, you see. Now Renato's given me a sister-in-law I do what she tells me as well. When Bernardo marries Angie I shan't know which way to turn.'

She choked with laughter, adoring him for his sweet temper.

'It's not kind to laugh at me,' he complained.

'I can't help it. You're a darling,' she said, and without thinking twice, she put her arms around him in a big, sisterly hug.

He embraced her back at once and they stood there, patting each other on the back and swaying slightly. The feeling of warmth and safety was delicious. Suddenly the world, instead of being a place she had to fight, became a refuge where she could dare to relax her guard because there was someone to take care of her. The weariness of days was gradually catching up with her...

'Helen—*Helen*—'

She opened her eyes. 'What?'

'You fell asleep standing up.'

She shook her head. 'I did?'

He grinned. 'I'm losing my touch. Women don't usually fall asleep in my arms.'

'I'm sorry. It's just that you felt so safe.'

'Don't add insult to injury,' he begged.

'I'd better get back to work.' But Helen didn't move. She felt held in a spell, with no power to break it.

Lorenzo made a sudden, resolute movement, thrusting her away and speaking in a theatrical approximation of 'macho'.

'Then do so, at once. That's an order, woman. This is a man speaking. Obey him.' She gave an unsteady laugh and he grimaced. 'Yes, I don't do it very well, do I?'

'You're out of practice.'

'I'll bring you some coffee.'

She returned to her books. The coffee duly arrived and she thanked him with a smile. When she next looked up it was to see Lorenzo washing saucepans.

She yawned and rose to stretch herself, still feeling sleepy. She stretched out on the sofa, meaning just to close her eyes for a few moments.

She awoke to find all the lights out except one small table lamp, and the front door opening.

'Hallo,' Dilys said, coming in, dressed to kill. 'I thought you'd have been in bed hours ago.'

'Why, what time—*two o'clock*?'

Lorenzo had left, she realised. Going into the kitchen she found it cleaned to within an inch of its life. Every cup and plate was in place. Every saucepan gleamed.

There was a little note under a fridge magnet shaped like a penguin.

You were sleeping like a baby so I didn't awaken you. Goodnight. Sleep well.

She smiled, thinking warmly of her friend's tender care for her. Then the smile faded as she thought of something else, and wondered if it was only her imagination that his lips had lain briefly on hers while she slept.

CHAPTER FOUR

ON LORENZO'S last day in New York Helen dropped into his room and found him deep in the throes of packing.

'Nearly finished,' he said. 'Now I have to see Fives to settle a few final points. Can you come with me?'

'I don't know, but I will anyway,' she said, thinking of the time to come when he wouldn't be there.

He was at Fives for an hour, spent another hour finalising the lease on extra warehouse space, and then he was finished. There were still three hours to kill before she would drive him to the airport. They had a snack in a burger bar, eating almost in silence. Suddenly there was nothing to say.

Central Park lay on their way back. After the bleak winter the trees were in bloom, glorious white and pink against the blue of the sky. He took her hand and began to walk slowly.

She wondered where they were going, but soon she realised they weren't going anywhere. For an hour they walked under the trees, hand in hand, and her heart was heavy. It was like the last day of the vacation, when you were still there but it was all over.

'I guess it's time to go,' he said at last.

She drove him to JFK and waited while he checked in for the evening flight from New York to Rome.

'There's a few minutes before they call me,' he said. 'Let's have a drink.'

He bought an orange juice for her and a scotch for himself, and they sat smiling, saying the things people say when they don't know what else to say.

'Have you got everything?' she asked.

'Too late now if I haven't. I've got my passport and tickets, so I won't go far wrong.'

'That's true.'

Silence.

'You've got better weather for going home than you had arriving,' she said valiantly.

'Well, it's spring now. Sicily will be beautiful. All blossoms.'

'So you're glad to be going?'

'I'm looking forward to seeing everyone again. But I've had a great time.'

'So have I.'

'Will you have problems with your family when I'm gone?'

'I'll just say we changed our minds. What can they do? Anyway,' she added on a teasing note, 'I promise to reveal nothing until you're safely out of the way.'

'Thanks,' he said with feeling. 'But seriously, I wouldn't like to think of you having trouble.'

'Don't worry about me.'

'I just hope Giorgio doesn't make himself unpleasant.'

'Giorgio's always unpleasant about something. If he shouts I'll shout back. I'm good at letting people know when I'm mad at them.'

'Yeah, I remember.'

And there they were, back in the first evening, with her saying she was good'n mad, and him not fighting back because that wasn't his way, and anyway he didn't have a leg to stand on. And they'd both known that the problem was the kiss he'd stolen, which was unlike any other kiss. And they'd also both known that the problem wasn't going to go away.

'Maybe they'll get to like Erik,' Lorenzo suggested. 'When they've forgiven you for preferring him to me.'

Preferring him to you? she thought. *Oh, you shouldn't have said that.*

'I'll be working with Erik from now on. In fact, I'll be joining him tonight at some hotel function.'

'Beware hotel functions,' he said with a grin. 'You meet some weird characters there.'

'I shall be quite safe with Erik,' she said primly. 'He's always the perfect gentleman.'

'Nobody ever accused *me* of being a perfect gentleman.'

He grinned again, and she wished he hadn't, because it made her realise how much she was going to miss his sweet temper and the sunshine he carried with him. This was really it. He was going away and she might never see him again.

'If they do, I'll put them straight,' she assured him.

Ten minutes to go.

'The important thing is that you're running your own life, not letting your parents run it for you,' he reminded her.

'With your help. We really outflanked them, didn't we?'

'We certainly did.'

Silence.

'Can I get you another drink?' he asked desperately.

'Just an orange juice, please.'

'Sure. I don't want to get you in trouble with Elroys. If you're meeting Erik I expect you need to hurry back.'

'I'll see you into the departure lounge, but I won't wait for take off.'

'No, no, of course not. I wouldn't expect— I mean, I know you're busy.'

'Yes, fine.'

'Fine.'

Silence.

'How is Erik about everything?' he asked

'Everything?'

'You and me—I mean, seeing so much of each other this last week?'

'He mentioned you when he called last night and said he was glad I was keeping a close eye on the hotel's interests.'

'That's all he said?' Lorenzo was outraged.

'Yes. Which is lucky.'

'Well, OK, but if I'd heard—I mean if the girl that I—if she—you're right. It's good that he's so reasonable. Sure. Right. Fine.'

Five minutes to go. Their drinks arrived. Four minutes. Time was slipping past and there was something she ought to say, but she didn't know what and soon it would be too late.

'I've got your email address, haven't I?' he asked for the tenth time.

'Yes, and I've got yours.'

'Stay in touch. Like we said—best friends.'

'*You* stay in touch. Let me know you arrived safely.'

'*Will passengers for flight—?*'

They got to their feet and walked the short distance. At the barrier they faced each other, smiling.

'Well, this is it. Goodbye—' he added provocatively, 'Elena.'

She made a fist and aimed it gently at his nose. He laughed and took hold of her hand, straightening out the fingers and dropping a light kiss onto them. Then his laughter faded and something seemed to have taken him by surprise.

She struggled to speak but nothing would come. She could see only Lorenzo's face and feel the warm pressure of his hand enfolding hers. Her throat felt tight.

'Goodbye, Helen. I'm going to miss you.'

'Goodbye,' she whispered.

Then there was his hand on her shoulder, his lips briefly brushing her cheek. As he walked away she could see the back of his head, easily visible above the rest of the crowd before a turning took him from her sight.

She stood amidst the teeming airport and felt more desolate and alone than ever before in her life.

She had said she would leave at once, but she needed a strong coffee, and she sat over it for half an hour before realising it was cold and ordering another. When she'd drunk that she told herself again that she should be leaving. But instead her feet carried her to the window from which she could see the 747 just starting to pull away. She stood rooted to the spot while it glided out onto the runway in the dusk, then gathered speed until it rose into the air and headed for the clouds.

Helen stared at the disappearing lights until she could see them no more. Suddenly everything was blurred and she wondered if there was rain on the window panes, until she realised that it was her eyes that were blurred.

It was a long flight to Rome and when he landed Lorenzo had a head like cotton wool. But he got straight onto the connecting flight to Palermo, and was home by the evening of the next day.

Renato and Heather were waiting for him, hugging him with delight and carrying him off home in triumph. There his mother opened her arms to her youngest son, her eyes shining with joy. Fede, the lover of her youth, now her constant companion, shook his hand. Heather hugged him again, although it was less easy now that her pregnancy was becoming obvious. Renato paid one of his rare compliments.

'You did a fine job over there,' he growled. 'The order books are overflowing.'

'And you've got something to tell, yes?' his mother asked eagerly. 'About Elena?'

'Mamma, it's nothing, I swear it. There's nothing to tell. We're just good friends.'

Baptista gave a little scream of outrage. 'You were kissing the first evening. You've spent the last week living in each other's pockets and *you're just good friends?* This is your Mamma you're talking to. Who do you think you are? A film star giving a press conference?'

'I didn't mean it that way,' he said hastily. 'We're just friendly, that's all. We had to work together a lot, and we had fun too. It didn't mean anything.'

'That's not what Signora Angolini says when we have talked on the telephone.'

Lorenzo tore his hair. '*Maria vergine!* Helen was right! Today Manhattan, tomorrow the world!'

'And just who is Helen?' Baptista asked.

'She prefers Helen to Elena. Mamma, can we talk about this later? I'm just glad to be back with my family. Where's Bernardo? Where's Angie?'

His mother allowed him to escape, but with a look that said she would talk to him later.

Neither Bernardo nor Angie was present. As Lorenzo had told Helen, his half brother lived a lonely life in Montedoro, the mountain village where he had been born. Bitter pride had made him reject the woman he loved because of her wealth. But great-hearted Angie had followed him, working as the local doctor in that comfortless place. Gradually he was learning to respect her, perhaps even letting himself love her again. But there was no sign of them at this gathering.

'Bernardo's vanished,' Renato explained. 'You know the way he's always doing that without warning. He'll be back in his own good time.'

'I thought he and Angie were sorting things out,' Lorenzo protested. 'Mamma, you remember your birthday party just before I left, when Angie wouldn't come in case the snow stopped her getting back up the mountain to her patients, and Bernardo left early? I thought it was because he wanted to be with her.'

'I'm sure he did,' Baptista said. 'When I called Angie that night, he was there in her home.'

'But it seems he left the next day,' Heather said, 'and he's still away.'

Before Lorenzo went to bed he emailed Helen about his arrival. It was meant to be a short note but he got carried away and found himself talking about Bernardo and Angie. Even at this distance she was easy to talk to and the words poured out.

He paused, wondering if he'd said too much. Would she really be interested in all this family stuff? But she'd said she liked the sound of Angie. He hit the Send button quickly, before he could change his mind, and tottered into bed, jet-lagged out of his mind.

Her reply was waiting for him next morning.

If you're fond of your brother, I won't tell you what I think of him for walking out on her—

'Thanks,' Lorenzo murmured with feeling.

—but if she's up there in the mountains trying to cope alone I think someone should check if she's all right. You say she's practically family. Isn't that what families do?

'I was going anyway,' he told the screen, with perfect truth.

His first day had to be spent closeted with Renato, talking business. But as soon as he could get away he drove up to Montedoro, arriving just as Dr Angie Wendham was finishing her evening surgery. She was beautiful in a blonde, almost fairy-like way, but he thought she looked tired and sad. She hailed him with pleasure and invited him to supper.

'I want to hear all about America,' she said.

He'd meant to speak about his travels, his triumphs, but all he could think of was Helen, and for the life of him he couldn't stop an enormous grin taking over his face.

'What's her name?' Angie demanded at once.

'I don't know why you women always jump to one conclusion. I spent some time with the daughter of family friends in New York. Her name's Helen and, before you hear wedding bells, I'm the last man in the world she'd dream of marrying. She told me that in the first ten minutes.'

Angie's eyes widened. 'You proposed to her in ten minutes?'

'She didn't wait for a proposal. She just rushed to tell me not to bother.'

'You don't mean you've met a woman who's immune to your charm?'

'If you like to put it that way,' he said, slightly piqued.

Angie chuckled. 'I like the sound of her,' she said, echoing Helen's own words in a way that gave Lorenzo an eerie feeling.

'Well, don't keep me in suspense,' Angie went on. 'Tell me—*ouch*!'

A fork had fallen to the floor and jabbed her foot. Lorenzo watched her bend down for it, then clutch the table. Alarmed, he made a dash and just caught her before she slid to the floor.

'I'm fine,' she said hastily.

'You look a bit peaky.'

'It's been a long, hard day. I didn't have time for lunch.'

He made her sit down while he prepared the supper. 'How are you managing?' he asked kindly.

She told him some of the story, but she still kept many secrets. Lorenzo could only guess what had happened the night of Baptista's birthday, when Bernardo had followed her up here, and why he had fled the woman he loved so soon after. But remembering how Angie had nearly fainted, he was beginning to think it was time he took a hand.

The next day he went looking for Bernardo in a deserted farmhouse where he had often hidden away before. He found him there again, and brushed aside Bernardo's protests. He had come to talk about Angie.

'I'm still your brother and I'm not going to let you screw up the best thing that ever happened to you,' he said, adding significantly, 'Things have changed. If you're going to add to the family, it's about time you started being a member of it.'

He left without receiving any promises from Bernardo, but as he jolted over the rough track, wincing at what this was doing to the suspension of his new car, he felt that he'd done a good day's work.

Suddenly he braked sharply, astounded by what he had seen under the trees. The next moment he was out of the car, staring across the track in a state of shock. For a searing moment he'd been certain he'd seen Helen.

There! Beneath the apple trees, standing in the orange dress she'd worn on the last day, laughing as she'd done then. He walked across and looked all around him.

There was nobody there.

He looked up and down the road, but he was quite alone.

Alone.

Suddenly he didn't like the sound of the word.

He wondered what she was doing now. New York was six hours behind Sicily, so she would just have reached work. She would be sitting at her desk, probably talking to Erik. Perhaps they would be leaning over some paperwork together, his fair head close to her dark one.

It was the blossoms that had done it of course. They had brought back the memory of how they'd walked, hand in hand, under the blossoms in Central Park. He'd tried to describe the beauty of his homeland in spring, and the memory had made him almost hallucinate her presence now. Yes, that must be it.

But he wished she might really be here with him, so that they could walk together, as they had done in the last hours before they said goodbye.

That night he emailed her, talking about Bernardo and Angie, but he left out his suspicions of a pregnancy in case it made her even more critical of Bernardo.

In her reply she said, *An odd thing happened yesterday. I went through Central Park on my way to work, and I could have sworn I saw you there. It wasn't you, of course, just a trick of the light.*

Lorenzo felt the hairs begin to stand up on the back of his neck, and tried to stay cool. Of course they were remembering each other. Nothing in that. And if, by sheer coincidence, her 'trick of the light' had come at about the same time as his own, that was no reason to start getting fanciful. He would tell her how he'd seen her under the blossoms, and they would share the joke.

But he didn't. Somehow he couldn't find the right words.

A week went by with no news from her. He felt aggrieved. They'd agreed to stay friends, after all. Besides, Elroys had made him her responsibility. It wouldn't hurt to call and remind her that it was her duty to keep in touch. Having decided on the right jocular note, he dialled her apartment, only to be met by an answering machine. Of course, the time difference.

He could email, but he had a strange desire to hear her voice, so he continued to call and to be met with the answering machine, for the next few hours. In the end he had to sit up until five in the morning. And then the phone was answered by a voice that made him drop the receiver as though it was red-hot, without saying a word.

Erik!

Erik was in her apartment at nearly midnight.

She'd done it, then. She'd used their friendship as a springboard to her own independence. By now she and Erik were probably engaged.

Great! Wonderful! He couldn't be happier! *Hell!*

But the next day there was an email from her. It was a light-hearted account of going to the movies with Erik and taking him home for a meal afterwards.

The phone rang while I was busy in the kitchen, and as Dilys was out I asked him to answer it. The caller hung up right away, but I know who it was.

Lorenzo groaned.

It was Momma. I'm sure of that because she called again later and Erik answered again. Of course I got lectured next day because he was with me so late. Why do people have such suspicious minds?

'Can't think,' he murmured.

He replied in similar light-hearted vein and for a few days they chatted about nothing in particular. If Erik's name cropped up more than he thought strictly necessary, at least she never again mentioned taking him home.

They exchanged family news. Giorgio had been cross when Lorenzo went away without proposing, and growled at her until Mamma told him sharply to shut his face. Criticising her daughter was a privilege she reserved exclusively for herself.

I know our mothers have been thick as thieves about this, she wrote. *I hope she isn't giving you a hard time.*

'Just now I'm having a rest from being told I'm a disgrace to the family,' he wrote back. 'Bernardo has returned and he wants to marry

Angie, but she's saying no. She's pregnant but she won't have him. Says he asked her for the wrong reasons.'

Helen's response was so like her that he could almost hear her indignant voice.

Good for her! If he only proposed because of the baby he ought to be boiled in oil!

He was incautious enough to respond, 'Helen, this is Sicily!'

Her reply was a sulphurous, *Exactly!*

After that she was busy taking her exams. Lorenzo called TransGift, an organisation that would arrange for flowers to be sent from a New York florist. He dictated the card, 'With love and best wishes, Lorenzo,' and ordered it to be sent with a huge bouquet of red roses.

But as soon as he hung up he though, Hell, no!

He called TransGift back and changed the roses to pink. 'And the card should read "With best wishes, Lorenzo."'

'Not "love"?' the receptionist asked.

'Not love.'

He replaced the receiver and sat brooding. Perhaps pink was still going too far.

He called back. 'Yellow,' he said. 'And the card should read, ''Best of luck with your exams''.'

'I'll do that for you, sir.'

But ten minutes later the doubts struck again. Yellow was a dangerous colour. He grabbed the phone.

'Yes, I've sent it through,' said the exasperated receptionist. 'But I'm in time to cancel it.'

'Are you sure?'

'TransGift is a very efficient organisation, sir. If you're having trouble with flowers, can I interest you in a teddy bear instead?'

'You do teddy bears? Great!'

'What expression would you like on his face? Romantic, macho, silly grin?'

'Silly grin. And a sash saying ''Good luck''. No card.'

When he put the phone down he felt as exhausted as if he'd put in a full day's work.

Helen telephoned him that evening. 'Thank you,' she said.

'He arrived then?'

'Yes, he arrived, and so did—'

'I thought of sending flowers,' he hurried on, interrupting her in his urgency to make matters clear. 'But flowers die. You'll be able to keep him, and every time you see him looking daft you'll think of me.'

'Well, that's true,' she said amused.

'Did you get flowers from—anyone else?'

'Erik sent me red roses, but like you say, they'll die.'

'I'm sure they're superb red roses,' he said, trying not to sound as nettled as he felt.

'The very best,' she assured him, 'bought from the hotel shop which will give him an enormous discount. I prefer Gigi.'

'Gigi?' he echoed, pleased.

'Well, you can't call a bear Lorenzo, can you?'

'It's not a bear's name at all,' he agreed solemnly. 'Anyway, the best of luck with your exams. Let me know how you do.'

When she'd hung up Helen sat looking thoughtfully at Gigi, who grinned foolishly back at her. He was five inches tall, covered in soft golden fur, and beautiful. She pressed her lips against him, then set him down beside the yellow roses that had preceded him by ten minutes.

Next to them were pink roses, and behind them a bouquet of red roses that cast Erik's into the shade. Laid out on Helen's desk were the three cards that had come with them.

TransGift weren't quite as efficient as they claimed.

The exams lasted three days and were gruelling. Helen was well grounded in all aspects of hotel management, both theoretical and practical, and she approached the first test with confidence. But it was much tougher than she'd expected and at home, that evening, she let out a long breath of dismay. From his new home on her dressing table Gigi regarded her with sympathy.

'You're coming with me tomorrow,' she told him. 'I need you.'

Strangely, the next day, she felt full of renewed confidence. Of course it was superstition to imagine that Gigi's presence in her bag was making any difference, but she sailed through the most difficult questions, and knew she was doing well.

When it was all over Erik said mysteriously, 'I'd like to take you to dinner next Monday evening. The Jacaranda, all the trimmings.'

'Have you come into a fortune?' she asked, astonished. 'The Jacaranda costs the earth just to go in the door. I'm honoured, but why not eat here at a discount?'

'Because a discount meal isn't good enough for what I have in mind,' he said firmly. 'There's something I particularly want us to talk about.'

This was worrying. Obviously Erik wanted to move their relationship onto a more intense plane, but she wasn't ready for that, and she couldn't think why. He was exactly the kind of man she'd always planned to marry, solid, reliable, not Italian.

At the other end of the scale was Lorenzo, light-hearted, probably unreliable, disgracefully Sicilian, but with a wicked ability to chime in with her mood, and a pair of merry blue eyes that seemed to get between her and Erik.

Which was nonsense, because they were just buddies. To prove it she told him about the planned evening in her next email. He responded at once.

'He's taking you to the Jacaranda? Boy, this must be some occasion!'

Yes, he says he wants to talk.

'So you'll be engaged to Erik in a few days?'

To which she replied with a frosty, *Nonsense!*

On the night she dressed up and he kissed her hand, smiling his approval. There were flowers on the table, and Erik's first action was to bring out a black box, with Cartier's on the lid.

'Open it,' he said, pushing it across the table to her.

The box contained a gold chain and locket. Helen regarded it with awe and dismay.

'Erik, I can't—'

'Wait, let me say my piece. I want you to have this for two reasons. The first is congratulations. You've done brilliantly in the exams. You'll hear officially in a couple of days, and I've put in a bid to have you assigned to me. The second is—well, it's rather difficult but there's been something I've been meaning to say to you—I've even thought maybe you guessed—well, anyway—' he took her hand between his '—here goes—'

She let him keep hold of her hand and heard him out in silence. With every incredible word her happiness grew. They spent a wonderful evening together, and by the time they left she was wearing the gold chain around her neck and a smile on her lips.

When she checked her computer that night Lorenzo was there, ready and waiting.

'So are you going to marry him?'

To which she replied simply, *Nope!*

Lorenzo considered that word for a long time. It told him nothing beyond the simple fact, and whatever had happened at the Jacaranda must have been more than the simple fact.

Friends told each other things, didn't they? She would tell him everything, if he just waited. Showing curiosity would be fatal.

So he carefully didn't ask. And she didn't tell. And after a week he realised, with deep frustration, that she wasn't going to.

CHAPTER FIVE

LORENZO sent Helen another little bear to congratulate her on her exam results. She thanked him, but then they were both submerged in work and the correspondence faded for a couple of weeks. He took it up again because he had big news.

'Just got back from a wedding,' he wrote. 'Angie and Bernardo finally tied the knot in Montedoro. He was going crazy because she wouldn't say yes, so in the end he asked Mamma for help, and we all turned up at Angie's front door and told her it was her wedding day.'

Helen's reply came whizzing back with the speed of light.

You kidnapped her and forced her to get married?

'Nobody forces Angie to do anything,' he responded. 'She and Bernardo love each other. They just got into a bit of a tangle.'

You mean, she didn't do what was expected of her, so she was manipulated.

'It wasn't like that.'

This time there was no reply, just silence. Alarmed, he seized up the phone, and dialled Helen's number.

'It wasn't like that,' he repeated as soon as she came on the line. 'We're all nuts about Angie. We couldn't just lose her.'

'I'm not going to listen to you,' she said firmly. 'You make it sound nice, but actually it just proves I was right all along. Angie should simply have walked out and left Bernardo standing.'

Four thousand miles plus an imp of mischief emboldened Lorenzo to say, 'In Sicily a woman just couldn't do that.'

He held the receiver away from his ear quickly. Even so her shriek of outrage reached him clearly.

'Martelli, you're so lucky you're the other side of the Atlantic!'

'I know. If we'd been face to face I'd have said, "*Si, cara, no, cara.* Anything you say, *cara*".'

Her chuckle reached him down the line, and made the hairs on the back of his neck stand up. Perhaps that four thousand miles really were useful. Otherwise he might have behaved in a way that would ruin their friendship for ever.

'Lorenzo—are you still there?'

'Yes, of course I am.'

'You went silent suddenly.'

'I was just thinking—'

'What about?'

'Um—what about? I was wishing you could have been there with me, and seen for yourself how nice it really was.'

There was a pause before she said quietly, 'Do you really?'

'Yes. I keep imagining how it would be if you saw my home and my family, and I could get rid of some of your tom-fool prejudices.'

'You'll never do that. My tom-fool prejudices and I come as part of a prickly package. Aren't you glad you escaped while you could?'

'Definitely. How are you?'

'I'm fine. Working hard.'

'How's Erik?'

'He's away at the moment.'

So he wasn't in her apartment, Lorenzo thought. He'd been straining to hear any background noise, but to his relief there was nothing.

'What time is it over there?' he asked.

'Eleven. I'd just gone to bed.'

'Sorry if I got you up.'

'That's all right. I never mind the chance to straighten you out on a few things.'

'Oh, it's me that needs straightening out, is it?'

'Sure is. It must be dawn in Sicily. Why aren't you in bed?'

'I am, with a lady friend snoozing gently beside me at this moment.'

There was a tiny pause before she said uncertainly, 'I don't believe you.'

He sighed. 'You know me too well.'

'Of course.' He heard the smile in her voice. 'Underneath that playboy exterior you're just Little Lord Fauntleroy.'

'It's a lie,' he said indignantly. 'A wicked slander.'

She burst out laughing and the pleasant sound was in his ears as they said goodnight and hung up.

He got into bed, expecting to sleep at once as he usually did. Instead, he lay in the darkness, brooding on something else that he would have liked to tell her, but couldn't.

Nobody had enjoyed the unorthodox wedding more than Lorenzo. At the reception he'd danced with all the prettiest girls, as his reputation required, and joined in the songs in his light, pleasing tenor. And, as one wedding begets another, he had especially appreciated the moment when his mother had announced her intention to marry Fede, the long-lost beloved of her youth, who had recently come back into her life.

But it seemed Baptista had another marriage in mind, and suddenly Lorenzo had realised that everyone was looking at him.

He'd jumped in alarm, exclaiming, 'Who, me? No way!'

They all smiled knowingly.

'Forget it,' he'd said firmly. 'I'll think about it in ten years. In the meantime, no way! *Do you hear me?*'

That made them smile even more.

And he couldn't admit to anyone—not even himself—that for a moment he'd seen Helen's lovely face, which was absurd because she was the last woman he would think of in connection with marriage. They'd settled all that the first evening.

The brief vision passed, he was laughing again, resolved not to think of it any more.

It was harder to ignore the memory of Bernardo's face as Angie had become his wife. After all their quarrels, all the pride and tension, they had claimed each other with the certainty of true love. Lorenzo saw and understood this with an insight that had mysteriously grown recently.

Later that night he went to his mother's room to kiss her goodnight.

'I think that all went very well,' she said.

'Yes, I was worried up to the last moment.'

'I wasn't. Not after Bernardo came to me and asked me to help him bring his marriage about. That was when I knew that, for him, Angie was *the one.*'

'How did you know?' Lorenzo asked impulsively. 'I mean, what's the difference between a woman's who's *the one* and—well—?' He wasn't looking at his mother, and a slight flush had crept into his cheeks.

'Bernardo is a very proud man,' Baptista said. 'And he discovered that Angie mattered to him more than his pride. When a woman matters that much, she is *the one*.' A gleam of mischief crept into her eyes. 'Perhaps one day soon, you too—'

'That's enough of that,' he said hastily.

'If you say so.' Baptista put her hand over his. 'I worry about you, my son.'

'Me? But I have a wonderful life, Mamma.'

'I know. Dashing here, there and everywhere, as a young man likes to do. But sometimes you seem to me—adrift.'

'Mamma, you're not going to arrange my marriage the way you arranged my brothers',' Lorenzo said firmly.

'I just thought you might have been arranging it yourself. Do you know how often you speak of Elena Angolini?'

'Do I?' he asked, alarmed. 'Never mind. You can forget her. She's practically engaged to a man called Erik. She says she isn't, but I'm not fooled. They'll announce it any day.'

'Is that why you're scowling?'

'I'm not. Goodnight Mamma.'

'Goodnight, my son.'

* * *

Helen reached the airport an hour after Lorenzo's plane was due to land. Her delay had been unavoidable, but she worried lest he was already through Immigration, looking around vainly for her, wondering if she'd let him down.

There was no sign of him in the crowd and she glanced up anxiously at the screen. To her relief the plane was so late that it hadn't even landed. She got herself a coffee and took it to the window where she could look out on the bright summer day, and the even brighter prospect of her friend's arrival.

It was amazing how often she'd thought of him, considering how busy her life was. By day she worked long, happy hours as Erik's assistant. In the evening she dated a variety of men. Some were young, some middle-aged; there were wealthy businessmen, impoverished medical students, the odd theatrical. They wined and dined and adored her, and they all bored her equally, for none of them made her laugh.

Before Lorenzo she hadn't known that laughter was important, but now every man seemed at fault because he couldn't show her the comical twist to a situation, or share secret jokes that excluded the rest of the world.

They tried to impress her with romance, offering flowers, gifts and verbal tributes. But such outright gestures only made her think of Lorenzo, whose words were either teasing or seriously confiding, never romantic, but whose eyes held an intense look she would sometimes surprise.

It was June. He had been gone for nearly three lonely months, and he might be away still but for the decision of the Elroy Company to expand.

'It hasn't been announced yet,' she'd told Lorenzo in a hurried telephone call, 'but they're buying up hotels all over the States. There'll be an Elroys in Chicago, one in Los Angeles, Las Vegas, and lots more. And all the contracts will be up for negotiation.'

'I'm on my way,' he'd assured her fervently.

In a little while he would be here. She would look into his merry face and the world would be bright again. She was smiling already at the thought.

But as an hour stretched to two, then longer, she frowned. At last she went in search of

Charlie, whom she'd met when she was trainee, detailed to meet important guests. She'd never known his last name, or his precise job, but what he didn't know about the airport wasn't worth knowing.

When she gave him the flight number, his face fell. 'There's a spot of bother with the plane. It can't get its undercarriage down. It's up there, circling, while they try to put it right.'

Helen went pale. 'And if they can't?'

'It'll land without the undercarriage. Technically that's a crash but it won't be too bad. Everyone will come down the chutes. Probably nobody will get hurt.'

In a daze Helen returned to the window, trying not to heed her mounting dread. Of course Charlie was right. Lorenzo would just slide down a chute and reach the ground safely. She tried to cling onto that thought, but now, her eyes sharpened by anxiety, she could see how ambulances and fire engines were discreetly gathering near the runway.

'Ladies and gentlemen, we apologise for the late arrival of flight—'

The words seemed to shrill along her nerves. Terror blotted out everything so that she hardly heard the next words.

'...*will land in the next ten minutes.*'

But what about the undercarriage? Lorenzo seemed to be there with her, laughing, giving her the wicked look that was so full of life and which she treasured. In a few minutes he might be dead.

She turned and ran to the observation area. There she strained eyes and ears frantically for the first sign. The news must have gone around for the place was crowded with worried-looking people who all stood in silence, gazing at the clouds. They were low today, concealing the plane long after it could be heard. But then it suddenly broke into sight and a storm of cheers and applause broke out.

The undercarriage was down.

Helen never clearly remembered what happened next. Her mind knew that she stood, held to the spot, while the aircraft descended to the runway, touched down perfectly and screamed away into the distance, before turning and taxiing back. She didn't move even when it came back into sight, gliding to its place and easing to a stop. All about her the crowd was erupting but she seemed locked in a block of ice.

She'd stayed motionless, knowing that soon she would weep tears of joy and relief, but just now she could only hold herself together, because if she didn't she would fall apart. She knew all this, but she didn't dare let herself actually think about it.

After a long while she told herself that she ought to wait for Lorenzo at the place where the passengers would be emerging, but her limbs couldn't move. This was all an illusion. The plane had crashed. He was dead. She would never see him again.

'Helen—*Helen*—?'

Lorenzo was standing in front of her, giving her shoulders a little shake.

'Helen?' he said again. 'Why are you crying, *cara*?'

A tender note in his voice as he said '*cara*' was almost her undoing, but she made herself be strong. 'I'm not crying,' she said quickly, brushing her face.

'When I couldn't see you I thought maybe you'd gotten tired waiting and gone home. I'm sorry I'm late. There was a bit of trouble.'

'Yes, the undercarriage. How much did you know on board?'

'They told us to prepare for a crash landing.' His familiar cocky grin was just a little frayed. 'Of course I knew everything would be all right in the end. They can't get me.'

'Yes—yes—I knew that too.'

The tears were coursing down her face again, and this time she didn't try to stop them. The next moment she was in Lorenzo's arms, having the breath squeezed out of her in a huge bear hug.

'I thought I wasn't going to see you again,' he said huskily.

'Don't say that,' she gasped, thumping his shoulders. 'How dare you scare me? How dare you?' Then she stopped thumping and clung to him, feeling him vigorous and solid, and trying to reassure herself that he was really here.

'I need a really stiff drink,' he said at last, in a voice that wasn't perfectly steady, and they made their way to the bar, holding on tightly to each other.

After three months he looked different. The Mediterranean sun had tanned him, making his curly brown hair lighter and his eyes a deeper, fiercer blue. Anyone seeing him for the first time would have known that this was a healthy male animal who lived through his senses and enjoyed it. Helen's heart was still thumping from the dread she'd gone through, but as she looked at him she knew there was another reason.

Not that that would stop her being mad at him for frightening her.

Once settled in the bar, they regarded each other suspiciously

'You weren't scared for me, were you?' he asked.

'*As if!*'

'I can see you weren't,' he said, sounding satisfied.

'I just thought how like you it was to be on the plane that fouled up,' she said crossly. 'You probably made it happen.'

So she was being unreasonable! So what? The relief from terror was so shattering that she was ready to lash out at him.

'Probably did.' He was watching her, a gentle smile on his lips.

'If you aren't the most awkward, worrisome, disruptive—'

'Disruptive? Me?'

'Well, aren't you? Don't give me that innocent look! From the first moment you came
into my life—sideways, let me remind you—
deceiving me, deceiving everyone—'

'Deceiving's a bit strong,' he objected
mildly.

'Well, it's your own fault. You've done
nothing but make my life difficult, kissing me
and letting my parents get the wrong idea
and—everything else.'

And haunting my dreams, she thought, *and
making me miss you every waking moment.
And then showing me the truth I don't want to
face.*

He held her hand for a moment, before saying, 'When I was eight I went off exploring,
the way kids do, and got lost. I was gone for
hours and they had the whole island out looking for me. When they finally delivered me,
wet and hungry, to Mamma—' he gave a soft
whistle '—boy was I in trouble!'

She looked at her hand lying in his, feeling
the warmth and strength that she might so easily have lost. Happiness seemed to be taking
her over, streaming to her fingers and toes,

bringing a silly smile to her face. She controlled it hastily.

'I think we should be making a move,' she said.

He seemed to come out of a dream. 'Yes—yes, of course.'

In the car he resolutely discussed his plans for the trip. 'A few days here, looking in on my customers, trying to keep them happy, then Richmond, Phoenix, San Francisco, Los Angeles, Memphis, Dallas, New Orleans.' He blew out his cheeks. 'I'm really going to be busy!'

'Are you going straight home from New Orleans, or coming back to New York?' she asked, carefully neutral.

He didn't answer at once. At last, he said in a strange voice, 'I'm not sure. Are you free for dinner tonight?'

'I think so,' she said, sounding casual, although it had been marked in her diary for a week.

'I'll meet you in the Imperial Bar at eight.'

She had a mass of work that afternoon but she got through it fast and was in the bar a few minutes early. Lorenzo's eyes opened wide when he saw the soft white dress she was wearing. A gilt belt clasped it in at the waist, and the V neck made the perfect setting for the chain and locket. She wore her black hair loose about her shoulders. He too had dressed up, not formally, but with the casual, silk-shirted elegance that made him even more impossibly handsome.

The sight of him made her heart skip a beat. But that was natural, she told herself quickly. The terrors of the afternoon had heightened her emotions. They would soon fade. But she couldn't repress a smile as she saw him, and her heart went right on beating fast.

'You haven't told me yet where we're going,' she said when they were in the taxi.

'The Jacaranda,' he said, grinning. Then he took her hand and said, 'You're beautiful.' But he saw her shake her head. 'What? What have I said?'

'You sounded like the others. I don't want you to do that.'

'Then I won't,' he said, alarmed.

Not until they reached the restaurant and were seated, waiting for the wine, did he speak again, saying severely, 'What's this about ''the others''? As a good brother I demand to know.'

'I like to be entertained in style, and I'm not short of offers,' she said lightly.

'Doesn't Erik mind?'

'Not in the slightest.'

'So what's the big deal with Erik? Are you two engaged or not?'

'I told you we weren't.'

'Yes, but you've also been mighty mysterious. What did he say to you that could only be said here?'

Helen's lips twitched. 'First, he wanted to give me this,' she said, touching the gold chain and locket.

'That must have set him back a few hundred dollars.'

'Nearly a thousand, actually.'

'Oh, yeah?' He sounded edgy. 'And you say you're not engaged?'

'It was a kind of goodbye and apology.'

'He's got someone else?'

'He's always had someone else. I was a ''front'' to fool the world—'

'The jerk!'

'—while he plucked up courage to "come out".'

Lorenzo stared. 'You mean—?'

'I've met the "someone else". His name's Paul. He's very nice.'

Lorenzo covered his eyes with his hand, struggling to control himself. He failed, and the next moment he'd burst out laughing.

Helen laughed with him. But behind the laughter she was musing on the things she couldn't tell him: the sudden seriousness in Erik's face as he'd said,

'I knew you'd forgive me, my dear, because it's been obvious to me for some time that you were in love with Lorenzo. You don't mind my saying so, do you?'

She had minded, but she supposed his mistake was understandable.

'Now I think of it,' she said, 'the way he courted me was always like a performance. Lots of romantic gestures, but he never really got close. I barely noticed because I didn't care about him that way.' She glanced up. 'Why are you looking at me like that?'

'I'm not,' Lorenzo said, hastily wiping the silly grin from his face. It was crazy but suddenly he could hear birdsong.

The waiter arrived with the wine, and soon as they were alone he toasted her.

'To your exam success,' he said.

'Thank you. I owe it all to Gigi. What a sweet thought. How did you come to think of a bear? Most people are conventional and just send flowers.'

'Conventional? Me? You know I never do what the other guys—' His voice ran down. Something about the gleam in her eyes, plus some worrying entries on a recent credit card statement, told him the worst. 'Did you—get anything else from me?'

'Only three bunches of flowers. And three cards.'

He groaned.

'I tried to tell you when we talked that night, but something you said made me realise you hadn't meant the flowers to arrive.'

'I thought they might send the wrong signals, so I cancelled them. But then I got my credit card statement and there they all were.'

Her lips twitched. 'I loved the cards.' A wild impulse made her add, 'especially the first one.'

'That one said—?'

'Love and best wishes.'

'Yes—well, you know how it is—in that sort of message—you say "love", but—'

'But what?'

'But—I don't know.'

'Neither do I.'

The silence was jagged. Helen looked up to find Lorenzo watching her, and everything they had tried to deny was in his eyes. She was back in the first night, in his arms, feeling his scorching lips on hers, growing dizzier, crazier.

But then she pulled herself firmly together. What happened that night had been a passing moment, and if she had ached for him ever since that was nobody's concern but hers.

'We may have a problem here,' Lorenzo said at last, speaking with caution.

'Not—necessarily,' she replied, trying to sound firm.

'Oh!' He sounded deflated. 'I thought maybe you—sorry, I didn't mean to embarrass you.'

'No, it's not that,' she said hurriedly. 'Of course I—it doesn't have to be a problem unless we let it. It's really only what happened this afternoon, me thinking you might be dead—'

'And me thinking I'd never see you again—'

'Exactly. That sort of thing makes people emotional, but only for a while. It doesn't *mean* anything.'

'Of course it doesn't,' he said resolutely.

'So if we're sensible, and don't get it out of proportion—not let it spoil things—'

'Fine. Ah, here's the first course. Looks good.'

After that no more was said on the dangerous subject. Helen didn't feel she'd handled it very well, and half hoped he'd bring it up again. When he didn't she felt depressed. But he didn't notice. He seemed rather depressed himself.

Three precious days in New York, so eagerly anticipated, seemed to shrink to nothing. There was a working lunch with Erik, at which Lorenzo was at his best, realising that he'd always misjudged this splendid man. There was a stream of visits to customers old and new. His mobile was never silent.

On the last night there was the unavoidable supper with the Angolinis, suffering under the broad hints of Mamma and Poppa and the impatient touchiness of Giorgio.

'I'm sorry,' Helen said in the cab on the way home. 'I'm sorry, I'm sorry, *I'm sorry.*'

'Don't worry. Families are a fact of life. But the least you can do is buy me a drink.'

Say no, warned her inner voice. *You're in a mood to be sentimental.*

'Anything,' she said. 'I think you're a positive saint.'

Elroys had its own nightclub, and a reputation for its music. Tonight there was a traditional jazz band, and they arrived to find the place loud and merry. They found a table in a corner, but it was too noisy to talk, so they took the floor and danced energetically for half an hour.

'I needed that,' Lorenzo said when they sat down. He fanned himself, breathing hard, and she did the same. The blood was still pounding through her veins in a wild, stomping rhythm, and she felt good.

The lights were low, and in the pink and blue shadows she could just make out his face, and the gleam in his eyes. She looked at him, storing up memories for the weeks alone. The last three days had tired her in every way. Three days of denying what they'd discovered at the airport, of pretending it wasn't true, of looking to the future with sad eyes.

He was regarding her wistfully and she knew his thoughts were the same, although she tried not to know it.

'I'm leaving early tomorrow,' he said. 'I'll be gone before you reach work.'

'I know. So we'll say goodbye now.'

'Yes...' A surge of longing had taken possession of her, making her heart ache. When he seized her hand and pressed it urgently against his lips she felt her control slipping. It was easy in the darkness to lean close to him so that when he raised his head his lips brushed hers, almost by accident.

'Elena...' he whispered, using the name he never used. *'Elena...'*

'Don't,' she whispered urgently.

'But you know...'

'Yes, I do. But there are some things it's best not to know. If we forget that—we could lose everything.'

'Or gain everything?' he asked softly.

She shook her head, and he sighed.

'I suppose you're right,' he said reluctantly. 'I just thought I'd ask my friend's advice.'

'Your friend,' she managed to say, 'doesn't want anything to spoil your friendship, the most precious she's ever known.'

If only he hadn't kissed her that first night. She felt she might just about cope without the memory of his lips scorching hers in a way no other man's had ever done. But her body had reacted instinctively, yearning towards him, wanting more, wanting *him*.

'I think it's time to say goodbye,' she said in a strained voice. 'You have to be up early. I don't want you to miss your plane because of me.' She barely knew what she was saying.

'I guess you're right,' he said reluctantly. He knew why she was running away.

They took the elevator up from the club to the hotel entrance. There was nobody else in it, and as soon as the doors closed he took her face between his hands and kissed her on the lips.

'I can't do that in the lobby,' he said. 'And I've wanted to kiss you so badly. We don't have to say goodbye—not just this minute—'

LUCY GORDON   133

She tried to answer but he was occupying her lips again with a kiss that tantalised her with thoughts of what might be. They were friends, she thought wildly, just friends. But desire was flowing through her, making a mockery of friendship. She wanted him to touch her everywhere, and to touch him everywhere. The craving for that was so urgent that she could almost feel his hands caressing her intimately, seeking her response. The sensation almost broke her control, and she clung to him, praying for common sense.

But common sense retreated in the face of her need to be naked with him, and to let him see her own nakedness. She knew she was beautiful, and what use was beauty unless the man you wanted could see it, and revel in it? In another moment...

They stopped. The doors opened. People were waiting to get in. They pulled apart hastily and hurried out. The moment was gone.

In the brilliant light of the reception area they parted.

'Goodbye, Signor Martelli,' she said, politely offering him her hand.

'Goodbye, Miss Angolini. I've really appreciated your help.'

'Please contact me if you need anything.'

'I'll be sure to do so.'

He was gone. She'd looked forward to this trip so much, but after a few packed days he was leaving for weeks, with perhaps the hope of another few days at the end of it. Then he would be gone again. For good.

She'd done the right thing. There was no doubt of it. When Lorenzo returned to Sicily there was no way she could go with him. Even if he'd asked her. Which he hadn't.

So she could congratulate herself on the wisdom that had saved her from making a dreadful mistake.

But why was it, she wondered forlornly, that the right thing felt so terribly, terribly wrong?

CHAPTER SIX

THERE was a queue at the desk of the New Orleans Elroy. Helen, shifting from one foot to the other, fanned herself against the heat and looked around the reception area, wondering if she'd been wise to arrive without warning.

She'd endured six weeks without Lorenzo, her loneliness broken only by his lively emails and a call when he could tear himself away from business. Again she was seeing the hardworking man who lived beneath the merry surface. She admired him for that, except when he had to hang up on her because a customer was trying to get through.

As he crossed the country she thought of him in city after city. When he reached Los Angeles she pictured him on the beach, his broad shoulders and handsome face drawing admiring female glances. There must have been plenty of those wherever he went, and the fact that he never mentioned women was somehow ominous. The truth was clear. He

135

was enjoying a frenzied orgy of decadence, and the sooner she found out the sooner she could recover her sense of proportion about him.

That was how she was explaining things to herself these days.

Now here she was in New Orleans. The idea had been taking up space in her mind for some days, and yesterday she had abruptly told Erik she needed some leave, and caught the first flight out. And as the queue shuffled forward she desperately wished she hadn't.

Then she saw Lorenzo.

The reality was so much like her imaginings that she briefly thought she was still dreaming. He was emerging from the interior of the hotel, his skin more tanned than ever, his look of vivid masculinity sharply emphasised.

With him was a young girl, of about eighteen. She was blazingly beautiful in a brash, flaunting manner. Her lush red hair hung to her waist, her hips wiggled, her young breasts were high and perky. Helen, who had slept on the plane in sensible travelling clothes, felt crumpled, rumpled and a hundred years old.

They looked as though they had come from the hotel pool. Lorenzo wore trunks and a short-sleeved shirt, open to the waist. The girl was dressed—sort of—in a wrap-around garment transparent enough to reveal the mini bikini beneath. And she was clinging onto to Lorenzo's arm as though planning to claim it as a souvenir.

Helen looked around wildly for somewhere to hide. He mustn't know that she'd turned up and discovered the truth like this. She couldn't bear him to know that she'd been such a fool. But he was so close now that any movement would attract his attention.

A middle-aged couple, immediately behind Lorenzo, were talking to him.

'Hey, Lorenzo,' yelled the man, 'we old folk are going to put our feet up. Why don't you and Calypso take that little shopping trip?'

And now Helen noticed that Lorenzo looked uncomfortable. 'I really have to be working, Mr Baxter,' he said, trying to disentangle himself from Calypso without actually pushing her away. He failed.

'I've told you, call me Dagwood.'

'I have to work, Dagwood.'

'Hey, what the hell! You've already taken a million off me. Relax. Have fun.'

'My girlfriend will be arriving any minute.' There was a desperate edge on Lorenzo's voice that made the sun come out for Helen.

'I don't believe you have a girlfriend,' Calypso teased. 'You're just playing hard to get.' She giggled. 'I like that in a man.'

'I promise,' Lorenzo said, 'Helen is real. And she'll be here.'

'You don't know that,' Dagwood bellowed cheerfully. 'Anyway, who needs her? A young guy should know how to enjoy himself, know what I mean?' He gave an ugly wink. 'Call her and put her off.'

'I think I will just—make a call.' Lorenzo freed his arm at last, and turned away from them into a corner, frantically pulling his mobile from his bag. Calypso shrugged and sauntered to the bar.

Helen inched close enough to Lorenzo hear the ensuing conversation.

'Elroys? Is Miss Angolini back yet?—You said that last time—but she *hasn't* called me— no, no, you don't understand, she can't be on leave—*Why?* Because I have to talk to her. It's a matter of life and death—no, it's more important than that—'

'Then you'd better tell me now,' Helen said, amused.

He nearly fainted.

'How did you get there?' he whispered, looking as though he'd seen a ghost.

Helen put her palms together, genie style. 'You rubbed the lamp, master, and here I am.' She became herself again. 'What is it that's more important than life and death or—' she cast a speaking glance at the Baxters '—can I guess?'

'Helen, you've got to save me. That girl's a piranha and she's got me lined as the next meal. I can't just tell her to get lost because her father is Dagwood Baxter of Baxter Consumables, and he's given me a huge order. So I have to evade her subtly.'

'Subtly? You?'

'All right. Save the funnies! I have an order that's going to make me look awfully good to Renato, but my virtue is under threat. I'm trying to protect them both.'

'Which one is more important?'

He gave her a baleful look.

Helen was enjoying this more every minute, but she concealed her amusement to say, 'She's little more than a child. What's her father doing?'

'Everything he can to push us together. She's the oldest eighteen you ever saw. She already has one divorce behind her. But to Dagwood Baxter she's still his "little girl". What Calypso wants, Calypso gets.'

'And Calypso wants you, hmm?'

'I've been dropping broad hints about my girlfriend, and calling you since last night, but you weren't there.' He sounded ill used.

'I wasn't there because I was on my way here,' Helen pointed out.

'You knew I needed you,' he said, deeply moved. 'And you came.'

'I didn't know, I—something made me come.' The air seemed to be singing in her ears. It was coincidence, of course.

Then irresistible temptation made her say, 'I just can't see you as a blushing violet. She's a beautiful girl. Why not enjoy the situation?'

For the first time she saw him angry. 'That's a stupid question,' he flashed. 'A really stupid, *stupid* question.'

They regarded each other.

'I guess it was,' she said at last.

'I'm glad we got that clear.' He was still offended.

'He's coming over.' Helen had seen Dagwood Baxter from the corner of her eye.

'Then it's time for action,' Lorenzo muttered, and the next moment she was being enveloped in a crushing embrace. '*Darling*, how wonderful to see you.'

His lips against hers made it impossible to answer. It was a practical kiss, given in answer to a desperate situation, and deliberately theatrical, to make a point. But underlying the theatrics was a serious intent that it would interesting to pursue later.

He released her slowly, muttered, 'Play up,' and immediately switched on a brilliant smile. 'Darling, let me introduce you to Dagwood Baxter, his wife Margaret and his daughter Calypso.'

Helen mechanically made a suitable response, aware that she was being looked over by the Baxter family. Calypso greeted her sulkily, while her father seemed taken by surprise. Margaret Baxter's manner was one of weary tolerance, as though her husband and daughter had become too much for her.

It was she who, seeing the storm on Calypso's face, suggested that the five of them have dinner together that evening.

'I'd have preferred to be alone with you,' Lorenzo confessed as they escaped afterwards, 'but at least it's better than being alone with that budding vampire.'

'You're scared,' Helen chuckled.

'You bet I am. I'm just a sweet old-fashioned boy. Mamma never taught me about girls like that.'

'I'll bet you found out for yourself, though.'

'I'm going to rely on your protection,' he said, side-stepping this.

'She won't be impressed by me.'

'She will if you do it right. At dinner to-night, can you manage ''clinging and possessive''?'

'With an effort.'

'Don't take your eyes off me except to look daggers at your rival. Act like I'm a lord of creation.'

'You're pushing your luck,' she told him frostily. 'I'll try, but frankly you don't convince me as a lord of creation.'

'That's right. Kick a man when he's down.'

'Don't tempt me. Anything else?'

'Yes. Dress sexy.'

'What kind of sexy?'

'*Sexy* sexy. So that she'll get the message and realise it's hopeless.'

'You conceited jerk,' she exploded. 'You impossible, self-centred, big-headed, puffed up, full of yourself—'

'*Will you do it?*'

'*Yes!*'

She had a lot of fun picking out her dress from the hotel's boutique. Her taste was excellent but tonight taste was out, and 'blatant' was in, so she chose a neckline that plunged in a deep V between her breasts and made a bra impossible.

It was cream silk with a skirt that came to just above her knees, showing her long, elegant legs. Gold belt, gold earrings and matching gilt sandals completed the ensemble. She knew a brief qualm as she saw herself in the mirror, but what the heck!

Lorenzo wanted sexy. She'd give him sexy.

She was braced for his reaction when he saw her, but not for her own reaction at the sight of him in casual evening gear. Lorenzo liked to live well and dress well, and he too had been exploring the hotel boutiques. Now he wore a beautiful white silk, embroidered evening shirt, open at the throat, just far enough to reveal a hint of smooth brown chest. It wouldn't be hard to see him as a lord of creation, she thought. But hell would freeze over before she let him suspect that.

'Will I do?' she asked lightly.

He drew a deep breath. 'I think—you'll do.'

She was glad now that she'd taken the chance. It was worth anything to see the awed look in his eyes as he regarded her.

'Then let's go into action, O lord of creation.'

Hand in hand they strolled through the hotel and out to the poolside restaurant where they were to eat. Their hosts were already there, and Dagwood immediately rose and took firm hold of Helen's hand, declaring that she must sit with him. As there was only one chair beside him this left Lorenzo no choice but to sit beside Calypso.

Helen had no problem sizing up Dagwood. He'd started with a small fortune and he'd built it up to a huge one, as he lost no time in telling her, then telling her again, and again. He was used to being able to buy anything and he expected things to continue that way.

His wife was more interesting. With no influence on either her husband or daughter she centred her life on her hobby, which was words. The precise definition of words, and the proper use of apostrophes, occupied her whole attention, and she had been known to stop a conversation dead in its tracks by expatiating on the subject. Her husband habitually bullied her to conceal his awe of her.

Helen had thought her own dress daring until she saw Calypso's which plunged low at the top and high at the hem, until the two plunges came perilously close to meeting in the middle. Lorenzo, she was glad to note, was conscientiously averting his eyes, despite Calypso's attempts to make this impossible.

Dagwood worked hard to divert Helen's attention from Lorenzo. He talked about himself, he made her talk about herself, he made her talk about Elroys, which she did dutifully until

Maggie asked her whether that was Elroys with or without an apostrophe. After that it took a while for the talk to get started again. Lorenzo addressed a remark to Helen and Dagwood promptly demanded how long they'd known each other.

'Since January,' Lorenzo said. 'We met under very unusual circumstances.' He nudged Helen. 'Why don't you tell them how we were discussing marriage in the first ten minutes?'

'I don't think that's a story for anyone else's ears,' she simpered, divining his intention at once.

Calypso was briefly diverted from her self absorption. 'You guys got the hots for each other *that bad*?'

Lorenzo couldn't meet Helen's eyes.

She controlled her amusement long enough to murmur, 'That bad. It caused a lot of problems.'

'OK, OK,' bawled Dagwood, not pleased with these reminiscences. 'Let's have some more to drink.'

Helen made another effort. 'Lorenzo's been telling me all about his trip—'

'I bet he hasn't told you everything,' Calypso giggled, snuggling against Lorenzo.

It occurred to Helen that she disliked Calypso very much indeed.

'I doubt I'd have been interested in everything,' she said coolly.

'In fact, I bet he ain't told you nothing,' Calypso said triumphantly. 'What?' This was addressed to her mother who'd muttered something in her ear. 'For Pete's sake, Mom! Who cares if it's a double negative? What's a double negative, anyway? We ain't feeling negative, are we, honey?' She was walking her fingertips over Lorenzo's chest.

That did it! Without altering her smile a fraction Helen leaned over to Calypso and said clearly, 'If you don't want to end up in the pool, take your hands off my man.'

'Daddy!' Calypso's wail almost parted the pool water.

Dagwood rose to his feet, almost frothing with rage. 'What's the matter with you people? You're animals. I don't have to take this. You!' He pointed at Lorenzo. 'You'd better get smart, right now.'

Lorenzo regarded him, his eyes sparkling with pure Sicilian anger. But his voice had a calm silkiness. 'And just what do you mean by "get smart", Mr. Baxter?'

Dagwood jabbed a finger in Helen's direction. 'She just insulted my daughter.'

'Actually, she didn't,' Maggie observed mildly. 'She said she'd throw her in the pool. That wasn't an insult, it was a threat.'

'Does it matter?' Dagwood was beside himself.

'Well, strictly speaking, if you—'

'Dammit, Maggie, this isn't the moment to start picking holes.'

'I was only trying to help, dear.'

Dagwood tried again. 'She insul—threatened my daughter. What are you going to do about it?'

Lorenzo rose, and there was something in his eyes that made Dagwood take a step backwards.

'I'm going to marry her,' he said flatly. 'That's what I'm going to do.'

'Then you can forget about selling your carrots to Dagwood C. Baxter. Yes, sir.'

Lorenzo's smile was full of soft menace. 'Mr Baxter—stuff your order.'

Dagwood snorted, gathered up his belongings, plus his family, and retreated with as much dignity as he could muster. At the last moment he flung back a look of loathing and was further affronted by the sight of Helen in gales of laughter.

When they were alone Lorenzo eyed her warily.

'You were marvellous,' she choked at last. 'The first man who's ever prized my hand in marriage over a million dollars.'

'Helen—'

'It's all right, I know you didn't mean it.'

'Of course I didn't mean it,' he said quickly. 'I'm not ready to die.'

'But I still think you're marvellous.'

'Yeah, marvellous,' he muttered. 'And a coward as well.'

'What?'

'Nothing. Let's dance.'

A band had struck up and dancers were whirling by the pool, now filled with the reflections of colourful shapes. Lorenzo took her hand and led her to where they could vanish into the crowd and be private in each other's arms.

He blew out his cheeks. 'Oh, boy, what an evening!'

'How are you going to explain to Renato that you lost a million dollar order?'

'I'll tell him to come out and try the lion's den for himself. Now forget Renato. I want to concentrate on that dress. It's been giving me problems. It's giving me problems right now.'

'I can see that,' she said, following his gaze down to her cleavage. 'You're behaving most improperly, and I think you should stop.'

'How the hell am I supposed to stop?' he said through gritted teeth.

She considered the matter seriously. 'If you were to draw me closer you wouldn't be able to see down that far.'

He tightened his arm. 'Like that?'

'That's better.'

It was getting late and the music had developed a more melancholy, reflective character, conducive to dancing closely. She shouldn't be doing this, she thought. She enjoyed the feel of Lorenzo's body more than she ought, and his mouth was dangerously close to hers, filling her with longing.

'How long before you have to go?' she murmured.

'I can stay here a couple more days. Can you stay?'

'Two days, yes.'

And then—nothing. For the rest of her life.

'I'll come back,' he said, reading her thoughts. 'And you can visit Sicily.'

'I don't think I should do that. People might get the wrong idea.'

'They'd think we were in love.' His mouth brushed hers as he spoke.

She tried to speak but his lips silenced her, and she knew that she'd longed for this since the first night, the first stolen kiss. The sensation was so ravishing that it almost stunned her.

At last she looked around and realised that they were alone on the floor. People were watching them, smiling. 'The music has stopped,' she said in wonder.

'Yes, and we're providing the entertainment. Let's get out of here.' He seized her hand and they hurried from the floor, to the accompaniment of applause.

At her door they stopped. *'Elena—'*

'Don't,' she begged. 'Just—go to bed.' She opened her door and half moved inside.

His whispered 'Goodnight,' was almost inaudible, but it stopped her. She stood for long moment, her head lowered, looking at his hand, resting in hers. She stepped backwards, still holding him, enticing him to follow her. He took a step, then paused, watching her face until she drew him after her and closed the door.

He reached a tentative hand to the light switch but she stopped him, and they stood in the semi darkness, listening to each other's soft breathing.

'Elena,' he said again, and she didn't try to make him say Helen. At this moment it seemed quite natural to be Elena, feeling her fierce Sicilian blood pounding in her veins and all her senses leaping towards him.

When he laid his lips on hers she leaned close, and suddenly the barriers were down and they were kissing each other with all the urgency they had tried to deny. It seemed such a long time since their meeting, and yet this kiss was only a continuation of that first one, as though they had been kissing ever since.

'We said we mustn't do this,' he murmured.

'We were wrong—so wrong—' She was kissing him madly, already wrought to an unbearable pitch of excitement just by touching him. 'This is something we—must—do—'

'Yes,' he said as his lips moved down her neck. 'I guess—we always knew that.'

She was distantly aware that his hands were moving, causing her clothes to slip away, one by one. She didn't know where her dress went, but without it she was wearing hardly anything.

'I must have been crazy asking you to wear that thing,' he gasped. 'It's been torturing me all evening.' He was tearing off his clothes.

She could barely see him in the semi dark, but she knew the width of his shoulders, and she enjoyed drawing her fingers over the hard muscles. 'Life guard,' Dilys had called him, making a joke of it, but as Helen savoured his power and beauty all laughter died in her, replaced by thrilling anticipation.

She had been so full of doubt, but now her doubts were fading to nothing, overcome by the magic of his caresses. This was Lorenzo, whose touch excited her as no other man's had ever done.

He drew her down onto the bed and eased off her panties, then looked at her for a long time, his eyes full of delight, a little smile of appreciation on his lips. Slowly he drew his fingertips down the side of her face and across her lips. It was the lightest movement but it filled her with fire, and she let out her breath slowly, relishing the feelings that were taking possession of her. He dropped his head to let his lips take over, touching her mouth softly, teasing it with intent.

Thus distracted, she didn't realise at first that his hands were on the move again, finding her breasts, caressing them with skilful movements that sent the warmth rushing through her. When he laid his lips against them it was almost a gesture of reverence, but it set off a tempest within her that blew away the last of her caution. She opened her mouth, luring him in and challenging him so that his own excitement mounted.

Her mouth, her face, her breasts all came to new life under his kisses, and she responded eagerly to the demands of his lips and hands. He had the body of a man who lived an active outdoor life, lean, muscular, honed to vigorous perfection. She could feel his strength but also his control and tenderness, his consideration and generosity, and her love flowed out to encompass him. This was right. This was how it was always meant to be.

She knew that at any moment he would move over her, and she was ready for him, eager. Wanting him with all her being, she reached for him....

The bedside phone shrilled.

'Oh, no!' she cried. 'Let's ignore it, until it stops.'

'*Cara*, I'm not a man of iron,' Lorenzo groaned. 'You'll have to answer it.'

'But who could want me at this hour?' she wailed in frustration.

'Find out, and get rid of them quickly.'

Helen snatched up the phone. 'Hello.'

'I must speak to Lorenzo Martelli urgently,' said a female voice. 'He's not in his room. Please, do you know where he is?'

'He's here,' Helen said reluctantly, and passed the receiver to Lorenzo while she slid off the bed.

She took her silk wrap from the wardrobe, pulled it on and went into the bathroom to give him some privacy. But she couldn't avoid hearing him say *'Carissima!'* into the phone. She closed the door, muttering Sicilian curses under her breath, mostly directed at the receptionist who had seen them together earlier, and must have directed the caller to her room.

As she splashed water on her face and tried to calm her shattered nerves Helen thought of the voice on the phone, with its soft, feminine vibrancy. It was a sweet, charming voice, and Lorenzo had said *'Carissima!'* with an affectionate urgency that revealed a lot. One moment he'd been tense at the interruption to his love-making. The next instant this strange woman had claimed all his attention.

'Stop this!' she told her reflection firmly. 'You're thinking nonsense!'

But her blood was still pounding in her veins with the heated anticipation that his touch had induced. Her whole body wanted

him wildly, and 'Carissima' had come between them.

When she heard the click of the receiver being replaced she went out, and what she saw
wiped her own problems from her mind.

'Darling, what is it?' she asked anxiously,
taking hold of his arms. 'Whatever's happened
to make you like this?'

She would never have believed that Lorenzo
could look so distraught, so ill. When he spoke
he sounded as though he were forcing the
words out through a daze of shock.

'That was Heather, my sister-in-law.
Mamma has been taken ill.'

'Oh, no! How?'

'She has a weak heart and she's had a bad
turn. She's had them before, but they're worried about this one. I have to go home.'

He shook his head as though trying to clear
it, and Helen put her arms right around him,
holding him in a wordless message of comfort.
He held her back, very tightly.

'She's been frail for years,' he said, 'but
somehow she always came through, and you
get to take it for granted that she always will.
But Heather's worried. She's so old—'

'Then the sooner you get home, the better. Get packed while I arrange your flight.'

'Helen,' he said suddenly, 'come with me.'

'What?'

He looked searchingly into her face. 'Come to Sicily with me. I'll need you there if—'

'Hush, it won't happen.' She kissed him lightly. 'But of course I'll come.'

He began to pull on his clothes while she picked up the phone to call the desk. But before she could speak Lorenzo reached out and cut her off.

'No,' he said, 'you mustn't come. Forget I said it?'

She looked at him in shock. 'You don't want me?'

'Of course I want you, but you have your job to get back to. What was I thinking of, asking you go half way around the world just to suit me? Forgive me.'

'What are you talking about?' she demanded. 'If you want me with you, that's where I'm going to be.'

'But your job, you've worked so hard and this is no time to be taking risks—'

'To hell with the risk. I'll talk to Erik, he'll help us.'

'You're wonderful,' he said simply.

Irrationally she felt tears start to her eyes. She brushed them away and called the reception desk. In a few minutes they were booked to New York, where they would connect with a flight to Sicily. Then she called Erik. As she had hoped, he was glad to help her.

'You'll need your passport,' he said. 'I'll get Dilys to take it to JFK.'

When she'd finished the call Helen sat still, trying to understand what had happened to her. Lorenzo was right. She should be concentrating on the job that had always been so vital to her. But all she could think of was him, and the anguished look on his face, and her need to comfort him.

CHAPTER SEVEN

HELEN'S first view of Sicily was very strange to her. It was the place that indirectly had affected everything in her life, including the person she had become. 'The old country' had been like an extra member of the family, issuing silent commands, the yardstick by which everything was judged, and against which she had always rebelled. And now here it was, a triangle of land floating in the midst of a glittering blue sea, and all she could think of was how beautiful it looked.

But she soon turned away. Lorenzo needed her now. He was pale and staring into space, counting the seconds as they descended, getting closer to the moment when some family member would meet them with the news—perhaps that his mother was dead.

Helen took his hand between both hers and squeezed it. He gave her a grateful look and squeezed back, trying to smile. His vulnerability touched her heart. For so long she'd tried to keep her feelings for him within limits, but the whole pretence was falling apart. She'd chosen to make love with him because her rising passion could no longer be denied. But this was more than passion. Her heart ached for him.

As they came through customs Lorenzo looked around him anxiously until he saw a young, fair woman, behind the barrier. She was waving, smiling, giving a thumbs-up sign with both hands. He dashed forward to embrace the young woman eagerly but carefully, for she was heavily pregnant.

As Helen grew closer she heard her say, 'It's all right, my dear. She's out of danger, and longing to see you.'

She glanced at Helen and he hastened to introduce them. 'Helen, this is Heather, who is married to my brother, Renato. Heather, this is Helen Angolini who came with me because— because—' he seemed unable to find the words.

'I understand,' Heather said quickly. 'Welcome, Helen. The family will be so glad to meet you after all Lorenzo has told us.'

This wasn't the moment to ask what Lorenzo had said about her. In no time they were in the back of the car, hurrying to Palermo and the hospital where Baptista lay.

'Mamma simply passed out,' Heather explained, 'and her heart rhythm became very unsteady. In view of her age we were worried. But the doctors have managed to stabilise her and she's looking a lot better.' She smiled at Helen. 'She was thrilled when I told her you were coming too.'

Helen smiled abstractedly, and left the other two to talk.

So this was Heather, the woman with the beautiful voice, whom Lorenzo called *carissima*. Helen could feel the glow of the affection and understanding between them.

In a few minutes they had reached the hospital and were ushered upstairs to the room where Baptista lay. Just outside it stood a man Helen recognised from Lorenzo's pictures as his brother Renato. He was a dark and swarthy, not as tall as Lorenzo and heavily muscled. He broke into a smile at the sight of his brother, and grasped his hand.

'Mamma has just woken after a good sleep, and she's well,' he said. 'Her first words were to ask about you.'

He opened a nearby door, pulling it wide, so that Helen had a clear view on the bed and the beautiful white-haired woman already looking eagerly to the door. Lorenzo went to her swiftly, gathering her into his great arms so that she almost vanished in his embrace. Helen caught a brief glimpse of her face, glowing with happiness at the return of her youngest, before the door was closed.

Renato was embracing Heather, giving her a look in which love and anxiety mingled. She made the introductions.

'We have all looked forward to meeting you, Helen,' Renato said, courteously. 'It was time Lorenzo brought you here.'

She wasn't sure how to answer a remark that seemed to imply so much. Luckily Renato's attention was claimed by the arrival of Bernardo and his wife, Angie. Again, Helen recognised them from Lorenzo's snaps.

More greetings. More keen glances as though her presence had some deep significance. The kindly Angie noticed her looking lost, and embraced her warmly.

'You came all this way to be with Lorenzo?' she said. 'That was wonderful of you. Some good news will do wonders for Baptista's recovery.'

'Good news?' Helen echoed.

'Of course I understand it's too soon to say anything officially,' Angie said. 'But we're all thrilled that Lorenzo has found you. I'll tell you a secret. I've been expecting this ever since he came home in April, complaining that you wouldn't marry him.'

'He—?'

'All he could talk of was you, and how you turned him down as soon as you met. And I thought then how clever you were because Lorenzo is a little too used to being chased. It was good for him to be unsure of you, and I just knew you were the one.'

'But—you don't understand—' Helen said urgently, 'I wasn't trying to trap Lorenzo. I'm only here to—to—'

Her voice died. Why was she here? Did any woman travel halfway across the world for a man unless he mattered more than anything in life? And hadn't she secretly known how her action would look to his family?

Apart from the joking reference in New Orleans, Lorenzo hadn't asked her to marry him, and she hadn't said yes. Now she was beginning to realise that question and answer were somehow already behind them.

Renato touched her arm. 'My mother would like to meet you,' he said.

She followed him into the room where the white-haired woman was half sitting up in bed, in the circle of Lorenzo's arm. At the sight of Helen she smiled and reached out to her.

'Miu fighia,' she said softly.

If Helen hadn't understood before, she understood now. Baptista had not only called her 'my daughter', but had done so in Sicilian, underlining the fact that Helen was no outsider but one of them. In the same moment Helen became aware that the rest of the family had followed her into the room.

'Signura,' she said, unsure of herself, instinctively responding in Sicilian.

'No, that is so cold,' Lorenzo's mother protested. 'You must call me Baptista. And you must let me thank you for coming so far.

Lorenzo has told me much, and I think you have a wonderful heart.' She sounded breathless.

'That's enough, Mamma,' Lorenzo said quickly. 'You're tired.'

'Yes, I am. There'll be time for talking later. For now, I have only one more thing to say.'

She reached out to an elderly man standing by the window, whom Helen had not previously noticed. He was tall and thin with white hair and a gentle face. He moved to the bed, looking down at Baptista with a smile.

'You know that Fede and I had planned to marry,' Baptista said. 'Now we will bring the date forward, so that we can make the most of the time that we have together.'

Her hand clasped in his, she looked up at the old man, and Helen drew in her breath at the love that blazed from their eyes, dimming everything else in the room.

The others were wreathed in smiles, congratulating the couple, eagerly making plans. Helen began to edge aside, but Baptista wouldn't let her hide.

'You will be at our wedding,' she declared, 'and our whole family will be together.'

Helen tried to say something, but no words would come. The tide was carrying her along at an ever-increasing pace.

Lorenzo stayed with his mother when the others left for the Residenza where the Martelli family lived. It was about half an hour's journey away, on a road that swung inland into deep countryside, before turning back to the coast

At last Helen saw the great house, made of yellow stone that glowed softly in the sunlight. It stood high up, overlooking the sea, a building of three stories, each a little smaller than the last, so that each storey was surrounded by a wide terrace, and each terrace was covered in blooms. Clematis, bougainvillaea, jasmine, oleander—the varieties and colours went on forever.

As she was led up to her room Helen had no time to take in much beyond a general impression that the Residenza was built in mediaeval style, with everything of the best. Tiles and mosaics lined the corridors. Broad staircases led up to lofty regions.

'It took me a long time to take it all in when I first came here,' Heather said. 'Now it feels just like home.'

'And you live here all the time?' Helen asked.

'Not all. Renato and I have a little estate called Bella Rosaria a few miles away. We live there a lot in summer, but we're here now to be near Baptista. Also our baby will be due soon. Here we are.'

She flung open the door to a huge room with two large four-poster beds hung with white net curtains. More net curtains hung at the floor-length windows.

Helen's luggage had already arrived, and a maid was unpacking it. She had almost finished the last suitcase and was holding the black velvet bag where Helen kept her few really good pieces of jewellery. The sound of the door made her look up, as if startled.

'What are you doing here, Sara?' Heather asked. 'I told Anya to do this job.'

'Anya had to go out, Signora,' the maid explained. 'I only meant to be helpful.'

'Very well, you may leave.' It seemed to Helen that her hostess was displeased about something. There was a coolness about her manner until the maid had left the room.

'Come and look at this view,' Angie said, coming in behind them and opening the windows onto a broad terrace. From here they could see inland, over the vast garden to the land beyond, stretching away to the misty mountains.

'It's beautiful,' Helen breathed. 'All my life I've heard about this country, but I never knew it could be so lovely.' She returned to the bedroom, out of the heat. 'This room—my goodness! It's—so much!'

'Yes, isn't it?' Heather agreed. 'It's where Angie and I slept when I came out here—' Something checked her.

'When you came out to get married,' Helen finished. 'Did Renato meet you at the airport and drive you back through all that wonderful scenery?'

When they didn't answer at once she looked around.

'No, Renato was busy that day,' Heather said quickly. 'Why don't you have a siesta? I'll send you up some refreshment. Lorenzo will be home later, and we'll all have dinner together.'

She gave Helen a small peck on the cheek, and departed

What am I doing here? Helen thought as soon as she was alone. *The one place I swore I'd never visit.*

But then Lorenzo seemed to be there beside her, giving her the smile he kept for her. Her body was warm again with the anticipation of his loving, her desire demanding to be slaked, her flesh aching with deprivation. And she knew that nothing could have stopped her following him while she lacked the fulfilment only he could give her.

Another maid arrived with coffee and sandwiches. She had them and settled down to her siesta. She was awoken by the feel of lips on hers, and opened her eyes to find herself in Lorenzo's arms.

'It made me so happy to know that I would find you here,' he whispered. 'What would I have done if you hadn't come with me?'

'But your mother is improving. You didn't need me.'

'I shall always need you, *cara*.' His eyes held a hint of mischief. 'We have unfinished business.'

She smiled back, teasing him. 'And when we've finished—shall I go home?'

He was suddenly serious. 'Our business will never be finished. Never as long as we live.'

He tightened his arms and kissed her long and deeply. She gave herself up to him, filled with a fierce emotion she'd never known in her life before. Even now she resisted putting a name to it, but she was where she wanted to be. How could she ever leave him?

He tore himself away at last. 'I was sent to tell you that dinner will be in half an hour.'

'That just gives me time to have a shower.'

'I'll come back for you.'

He did return, just as she'd finished slipping into a deep blue dress that looked ravishing against her dark colouring. But he wasn't alone. Helen heard him chatting with someone as they approached, and opened her door to see him standing there with his arm about Heather's shoulders.

'We came to fetch you,' Heather said, smiling in her friendly way.

In Baptista's absence Heather was the lady of the house. She took Helen's hand and personally led her downstairs to where the family was gathering for the evening meal, underlining the consensus that this stranger was already one of them.

Renato also made the matter plain by saying, 'I've had Dagwood Baxter burning up the lines, cancelling that million-dollar order the day after he placed it. How come?'

'I told him to stuff it,' Lorenzo replied.

'Why?'

'He insulted Helen.'

'In that case you did right,' Renato said at once.

It was like that for the rest of the evening, warmth, kindness, acceptance. Helen blamed herself for a slight apprehension, but it was rooted in a deep instinct, and she couldn't help it. But it would pass, she assured herself. All would soon be well.

The wedding of Fede and Baptista was planned quickly, but with the Martelli genius for organisation. Fede's son by his first marriage would arrive from Rome the day before, and his son would be best man. His daughter sent her love but was unable to be present, as her little boy was poorly.

Helen was there on the evening after Baptista returned from hospital, when the family discussed who would give the bride away? Renato and Lorenzo squabbled amiably for the honour. Bernardo, not being Baptista's son, made no claim, but to Helen's eyes his air of unconcern wasn't quite convincing. Gradually the truth dawned on the others too, and a silence fell.

'Why don't you all three do it?' Helen asked. 'It's easy, really. Two of you take an arm each, and the third leads the way.'

'What a wonderful idea,' Baptista said at once. 'I shall be escorted by *all* my sons.'

There was a general air of relief. Afterwards Angie hugged Helen, whispering, 'Thank you.' Lorenzo winked and gave her a thumbs-up of approval, and Baptista took her hands saying happily, 'Already you are one of us.'

At that there were more nods and smiles, but the conversation passed on to something else before Helen could speak. So there was no chance for her to say, 'But I'm not one of you. I never can be.'

Even if she could have brought herself to say it.

That night she and Lorenzo walked on the terrace overlooking the sea, glorious in the moonlight.

'My mother really loves you,' he said. 'You made her so happy with that idea. In fact you made us all happy. Bernardo's a thorny character, but you seem to have found the key to him. Has Mamma told you yet that she wants you to be her attendant?'

'What about Heather and Angie?'

'They're both heavily pregnant. Especially Heather.'

'But I'm not one of the family.'

'Well, you soon will be.'

Now was the time to say, 'I can't marry you.' Instead she let him draw her into the circle of his arms, and his kiss blotted out everything else.

Everything was different now. 'Unfinished business', Lorenzo had called it, and she couldn't be with him without remembering how close they'd come to physical delight. Her body yearned towards him as much as her heart. But what could be arranged so easily in New Orleans was impossible here in the respectable house of Baptista Martelli. Unless they married...

She shut that thought off. Of all the foolish reasons for marrying a man the desire to make love with him made the least sense in this day and age. It didn't matter that the sight of him filled you with happiness and anticipation, that his touch sent tremors of delight through you, and the sound of his voice melted your heart. It didn't matter that you awoke thinking of him and went to bed aching for him, or that you couldn't picture life without his wicked, teasing smile.

You put these things aside because he was Sicilian, and you'd sworn—long ago, in the days before you lost your wits—that you would never marry a Sicilian. So any day now you were going to reject him and walk out of his life.

But not yet—not quite yet—

The morning after Baptista's return she asked Heather to join her over coffee. Apart from her

own approaching nuptials her chief interest
was the birth of her first grandchild.

'How are you?' she asked Heather as they
sat together on the wide terrace overlooking
the sea. 'I remember the last few weeks are
very tiring. And you've had to take on the running of this house while I was away.'

'Mamma,' Heather protested, 'the house
runs itself. But I'm afraid I've had to dismiss
Sara for stealing.'

'Has she started that again?' Baptista said
with a sigh. 'I caught her once and allowed her
to stay because she promised it wouldn't happen again. But I suppose she broke her word.'

'I know she took things of mine, only trin-
kets, but she had her eyes on Helen's jewellery.'

'You were right to send her away. Now let
us think of more pleasant matters. Elena has
agreed to be my attendant at the wedding and
so—' her face brightened '—Elena, *cara*, we
were just talking about you. And Angie. Let
us all have lunch together.'

The next couple of hours were very pleasant
as the four women relaxed on the terrace in
the sun, and chatted dreamily about the im-

mediate future. After lunch Baptista retired for her afternoon nap, while Heather and Angie also voted to put their feet up for a while.

Heather courteously apologised for leaving her guest alone, and Helen assured her that she was perfectly happy. But the truth was that this sleepy way of living was irksome to someone of her energetic nature. She was saved from an afternoon's boredom by a phone call. It was Erik.

He came straight to the point. 'You can be very useful to the company. Do you know the Castella di Farini?'

'The great palace in Palermo? Yes.'

'Elroys is buying it to convert into an hotel. The deal is almost complete but at the last minute the owner is being tiresome about a detail. Our American lawyers out there don't understand Sicily. Our Sicilian lawyers don't understand Elroys. You've got a foot in both camps, and you might be able to sort it. Here's what you do....'

Helen made notes eagerly as she realised that this was a problem she could deal with.

'Leave it to me,' she said at last.

She almost skipped out of the house and headed for the garage just as Lorenzo's car appeared. 'What's the rush?' he called cheerfully. She hurriedly explained. 'Get in. I'll drive you there.'

'Erik says I've got a foot in each camp,' she elaborated as they headed for Palermo. 'Which means he's another one who thinks I'm more Sicilian than I am—why are you laughing?'

'That's the first time I've heard you admit you're even part Sicilian. We'll get you yet.'

'I'd thump you if you weren't driving,' she said amiably. 'It's just that Erik might expect more from me than I can deliver. Not that I told him that. I let him think I was all confidence.'

'Good for you. Do you want me to come in too?'

'No, thank you, *caro*,' she said firmly. 'I appreciate the offer, but I don't want him going soft on me just because I've got Martelli backing. I'll do this on my own.'

Suddenly she was alert, pointing out of the window at a building that stood on a small incline. It seemed to be early nineteenth century, magnificent, and in good condition. 'Lorenzo, what is that place? Who owns it?'

'The city. It's the Palazzo Lombardi. It's being renovated to be a museum. It's quite a place. It used to belong to—'

He chatted easily about the building until they reached Palermo and pulled up outside the Castella di Farini.

'Shall I wait for you?' he asked, 'or would that compromise your independence?'

'I think it might. I'll get a cab. But thank you anyway.'

The owner was waiting for her, wreathed in smiles. He showed her over the magnificent building, and Helen loved every inch of it. It was far too grandiose for modern living, but it would make a wonderful hotel. Ideas began to dance through her head.

The difficulty he had raised was trivial, little more than a tactic to up the price. Over a glass of wine Helen smiled and indicated that if he'd changed his mine about selling, there was really no problem. The Elroy Company had its eyes on the Palazzo Lombardi, which might suit better.

The owner's fixed professional smile wavered a fraction. Helen met it with a fixed professional smile that didn't waver at all. In half an hour she had left the building, heading for the Ufficio Postale where there were telephones.

'It's sorted,' she crowed to Erik. 'But I took such a risk.' She told the story and Erik rocked with laughter.

'Excellent. One up to your local knowledge.'

'But if it hadn't worked you'd have fired me.'

'Probably. But it did work, and I'm admiring your skills. You need to talk to Axel Roderick. He's going to be the manager.'

She called Roderick's New York number and they talked for half an hour. He was pleasant and encouraging, asked her to do a few more things to help prepare the ground, and to meet him at the airport when he arrived the following week. She hung up feeling triumphant, and took a cab back to the Residenza, where she found Lorenzo sitting on the steps outside, looking worried. He smiled as soon as he saw her.

'The others are all having dinner inside,' he said, kissing her.

'Lorenzo, I'm sorry—'

'No problem. I explained.'

Over dinner she described her afternoon, and they all listened with approval, although Renato said, 'The city council will never part with the Lombardi. Lucky for you he didn't know that.'

'He did,' Helen replied. 'But I told him not to count on it because it was never wise to mess with Elroys.'

Angie chuckled. 'You're a real little Machiavelli.'

'Don't say that,' Helen protested in dismay.

'It's a compliment,' Renato assured her. He clapped his brother on the shoulder. 'Lorenzo, you're going to have to mind your manners with this lady.'

There it was again, the assumption that she was here to stay, part of the family. It was kind, yet she couldn't escape the feeling that a fetter had been laid on her: a silken fetter, hung with flowers and kisses, yet a fetter nonetheless.

But hadn't she herself taken the first step that very afternoon? The Hotel Elroy of Palermo! Could the Martellis be blamed for seeing where the signposts led?

CHAPTER EIGHT

AXEL Roderick was a plump, easy-going man in his fifties, a hard worker and an able administrator but chiefly a good company man. His aim in life was to impress his employers, and he was happy to rely on the efforts of others. By the time Helen had driven him from the airport and expounded her ideas over dinner he was convinced that this imaginative, energetic young woman was the answer to his prayers. He offered her the job of his personal assistant, and she gladly accepted it. Now she could stay in Sicily 'long enough to decide about Lorenzo'. That was how she put it to herself.

With the last difficulty out of the way the sale went through quickly, and renovations began. Helen was due to take up her new job the week after the wedding of Fede and Baptista.

It was to take place in Palermo Cathedral, not the vast main body of the church, but a tiny side chapel, private to the Martellis.

Helen arrived first, with Angie and Heather, and while they went ahead she waited for the second car bearing the bride and her three sons. Baptista was magnificent in pale grey silk, adorned only by a pearl necklace, Fede's wedding gift.

Helen handed Baptista her bouquet, then slipped in behind the bridal party, as they approached the chapel.

It was surely the most extraordinary wedding Palermo cathedral had ever seen. When it was time to give the bride away three tall, handsome young men stepped forward. And the tallest and handsomest by far, Helen thought, was Lorenzo.

Baptista's elderly face glowed into beauty as she became the wife of her one true love. She had waited forty years for this. They had been full years, yet Helen had the strangest feeling that only in this moment had Baptista's life really started. And the same was true of the man whose love for her had never abated in all the long time apart.

She looked up to find Lorenzo watching her. He was smiling, not with his mouth but with his eyes, and that smile seemed to reach out and encompass her, drawing her into his heart, into his life, forever. He was telling her that this was where she belonged, and her heart was singing that he was right.

Afterwards there was a small reception at the Residenza, with a cake that had nearly cost Baptista's cook a nervous breakdown. There were toasts and speeches, including a brief one from Fede, who, as always, seemed a little shy. Afterwards Helen sought him out. From the start she had been drawn to the quiet, elderly man who said little but seemed to see everything.

'I feel a little overwhelmed by the family,' she said. 'Although they are wonderful to me.'

'And to me also,' he confessed. 'But I too sometimes feel overwhelmed.'

'Won't that make things a little difficult for you?' she ventured, for it had been decided that Fede was to live in the Residenza. He had given up his little home in Palermo, and signed over his flower business to his children.

He gave his sweet smile. 'I know what you mean. Of course I shall have a pension from my business. Even so, were I a much younger man I would not consent to such an arrangement. But at my age you find that the things that once seemed so important fall away. Only love is left. Only love has really mattered all the time.'

'That's very true,' Lorenzo said from just behind Helen. He shook Fede's hand. 'We're all glad to have you in the family.'

Fede thanked him, but not without a little smile at Lorenzo's unconscious assumption that the bride's family had absorbed the groom, rather than the other way around. Helen nodded, understanding his thoughts, but also understanding why these things weren't of such vital importance. Only love mattered.

'What is it?' Lorenzo asked, taking her hand.

'Nothing. This is all so nice.'

'I thought you didn't like families,' he teased. 'Especially this kind of family. Pity, because they're over the moon about you.'

'I feel the same way about them, it's just—'

With that swift intuition that was one of the loveable things about him, he divined her thoughts. 'You've got your job. You'll still have everything you've worked for.'

'You make it sound so easy,' she murmured.

'It is, if we love each other. I spent a lot of time pretending I wasn't in love with you, but you weren't fooled. Not really.'

'Not really,' she agreed.

'You know what I want. Don't you want it too?'

A bright carpet of flowers was spread before her, tempting, lovely. But it led out of sight, to a future she must take on trust. If only....

Then she became aware of the silence. Looking around, she saw that everyone was watching them, as though following each softly spoken word.

And then Lorenzo did the unforgivable thing, the thing that disarmed her, set her defences at nothing, and destroyed all her good resolutions. In the sight of them all he went down on one knee before her and said, 'Elena, will you marry me?'

'Get up,' she said frantically.

'Not until you promise to marry me.'

'Then you'll stay there for ever.'

'OK, if I stay here forever will you marry me?'

And suddenly everyone was clapping and cheering and Lorenzo was on his feet, kissing

her exuberantly and she seemed to have said
yes, although she never recalled saying it. But
you couldn't reject a man who'd knelt before
you in front of his whole family. Could you?

When Helen looked back on her first weeks in
Sicily they seemed to be full of dramas with
no time to breathe between them. After
Baptista's illness came her wedding. And
while they were all celebrating the engagement
of Helen and Lorenzo, Heather's child was
born.

It was an unexpectedly difficult birth that
took far longer than it should have done. For
a while everyone had a bad scare. and it took
a long night of pacing hospital corridors fear-
ing the worst before the clouds lifted. Helen's
chief memory of that night was of Renato,
standing apart from the rest, his face like stone.
There was no clue to how his wife's danger
affected him. No hint of love, or any kind of
feeling.

It was Lorenzo who showed his emotion,
holding onto Helen's hand as they sat together.
There were tears in his eyes, and when Renato
was summoned in to be with his wife Lorenzo

stared anxiously after him. An hour later Renato emerged to say that Heather had given birth to a healthy son, and was out of danger. The whole family erupted, but it was Lorenzo who jumped up to punch the air, and the next moment Helen was having the life squeezed out of her with a bear hug while he laughed with joy and the tears poured down his face.

She held onto him, laughing and crying too, and wondering how she could ever have pretended to herself that they didn't love each other.

On the day Heather returned home they had a moment together, and Helen observed ruefully that she felt as though she was already a family member and always had been.

'That's true,' Heather agreed. 'The Martellis take possession of you from the first moment.'

But she said it with a happy smile and it was clear that she liked it this way. Heather's experience had been the opposite of Helen's, as she disclosed in a cosy chat. She had no brothers or sisters, had lost her parents early, and fallen happily into the Martellis' open arms. Mostly she and Renato lived in Bella Rosaria, the estate that Baptista had given to

her. But for the birth of her child she'd returned to the Residenza, and was totally happy
sharing a roof with the mother-in-law who
adored her.

For Helen, seeking to escape the suffocating
embrace of family expectations, it was different. She envied Angie and Bernardo, living in
their mountain retreat of Montedoro, where
Angie was a doctor and very much her own
woman.

To her relief Lorenzo instantly agreed that
they should have a home of their own, and
they spent happy hours hunting for a house
small enough for two, yet large enough for a
man who'd been reared in a the huge
Residenza. They found a charming little villa
in Palermo, near the harbour, and rented it at
once, with an option to buy later.

'They say we can buy the furniture too,'
Lorenzo murmured with a questioning eye on
his bride-to-be.

'Hmmm!' she said cautiously.

'Hmmm?'

'Nah!'

'Thank goodness,' he said, with a sigh of
relief. 'We'll get some of our own, but it'll

have to be later because Renato's keeping me hard at it while he's "got the use of me" as he puts it. In fact I have to make for the airport now.'

'And I can't even see you off to France. I've got a dozen people coming this afternoon and I can't leave anything to my secretary.'

'What about Axel?'

She chuckled. 'Axel's a dear, but his idea of hard work is to pat me on the head and say, "You do it your way, sweetie".'

'Hm! As long as that's all he pats. Bye, *cara*.'

The Martelli clan had taken it for granted that the wedding would be as soon as possible.

'While the weather is still good,' Baptista had pointed out. 'Soon it will be autumn.'

Helen, who'd thought perhaps she would take it slowly and get to know Lorenzo in his home background, had found herself conceding. She couldn't have explained a delay in any terms they would have understood.

With so much to do in her job she had little time for wedding preparations, which suited her prospective in-laws perfectly. Angie too had moved in to the Residenza for the last weeks of her pregnancy, leaving her medical practice in the hands of her brother who had come out from England.

When Helen returned home from work they would all raise their heads from what they were planning, and call, 'Come and see this.' Their arrangements would always be perfect, and it would have been unkind to cry, as she sometimes wanted to, 'Not so much.'

Only once did she voice her thoughts, one afternoon when she, Heather and Angie were sitting together in the gardens of the Residenza, enjoying the autumn sun glittering on the fountain. Before them, on a small table, were coffee and cakes.

'Sometimes,' Helen said wistfully, 'I wish my wedding could be like yours, Angie. All arranged at the last minute, with just your close family in the village church. As it is—' she sighed.

'Yes, you are getting a bit swamped,' Angie agreed sympathetically. 'Palermo cathedral, *and* the *Jubilate*.'

This made them all laugh. Piero Vanzini, a local musician, had composed a *Jubilate* which he was anxious to hear performed, so he had obtained permission to play it at the wedding, and was rehearsing the choir to exhaustion point.

'And practically every relative in the whole world,' Angie finished.

'My whole family from New York,' Helen said. 'It'll be lovely see Mamma and Poppa, and my brothers and sisters, but there'll also be fifty thousand others, including some I'm pretty sure we're not related to at all. They've practically chartered the plane. And, of course, Giorgio.' She made a face.

'You really don't like him, do you?' Heather chuckled from the rustic chair where she sat with little Vittorio in her arms.

'No, I don't like him at all,' Helen said. 'He thinks now that his sister-in-law is marrying a Martelli his family over here is going to have it easy. He's already telephoned me twice demanding to that I should ''use my influence'' for them. But Lorenzo says their produce just isn't good enough.'

'Then let Lorenzo tell him,' Heather suggested.

'No way,' Helen said at once. 'I can deal with him without having to call for male assistance.'

'Don't be so prickly,' Heather laughed. 'I only meant that Lorenzo has a lot of firmness under that boyish charm.'

'So do I have a lot of firmness,' Helen said. 'Leave Giorgio to me.'

But the other two were smiling at her, and in the pleasant afternoon sun it was easy to let her indignation slip away. Helen had been looking through the photos of Angie's mountain wedding, appreciating its simplicity and the spontaneous happiness on everyone's face.

Angie's dress had been a soft cream silk with a tiny veil, held in place by yellow roses. It had been one of three that Heather had hired to take up to Montedoro, a neat arrangement that struck Helen as nicer than standing for hours being fitted for an extravagant creation.

Her glorious bridal gown was Baptista's gift, a sign that her future mother-in-law wished to do her honour, and Helen appreciated that. But she felt increasingly suffocated by the tide of finery that signified she was a Martelli bride, and which she knew would send her mother into transports of delight.

'What are you thinking?' Angie asked, watching her face.

'Of my mother, and what she'd say if she could see us now; one new mother, one almost mother, and me in the countdown to my wedding *in Sicily*, to a *Sicilian*. After all I've said in the past. Of course, Mamma would insist that I'd finally ''seen sense''.'

'And that would make you so mad,' Angie chuckled.

'Yes, it would,' Helen said ruefully.

If only, she thought, it could be just Lorenzo and herself. But he was still in France, garnering orders that must be in place before he could leave on their honeymoon. Helen understood this, but she increasingly felt as though she were marrying a phantom.

With three days to go she put in her final afternoon at the hotel. When she returned in three weeks she would be Signora Martelli. Axel kissed her jovially, gave her a costly gift for the new house and told her he hoped she wouldn't get seasick, a reference to the honeymoon which was to be spent cruising on Renato's boat, the Santa Maria.

It was a lovely day, and instead of going straight home she wandered down to a spot overlooking the harbour, where she could just make out the great mast of the *Santa Maria*. She thought of the honeymoon, when they would be alone, except for the crew, free to please each other and only each other. Unfinished business, she thought, with a smile.

Turning away, she collided with someone who'd been standing just behind her, and saw her go sprawling on the hard ground.

'I'm sorry,' she said, going down on her knees to assist her victim. 'Are you hurt.'

The young woman was rubbing her elbows, but didn't seem injured.

'It's not so bad,' she said. Then she grew suddenly alert as she saw who had knocked her down. At the same moment, Helen's eyes brightened with recognition.

'It's Sara, isn't it?' she asked. 'Here, let me help you up.'

When they were both back on their feet and had recovered the oranges that had rolled out of Sara's bag, Helen resumed, 'Didn't you used to work at the Residenza?'

'That's right.'

'Let me buy you a cup of coffee to make up for hurting you.'

They found a little bar and Helen bought them both coffee and cakes.

'You left very suddenly,' Helen remembered. 'Did you have another job to go to?'

Sara shook her head, apparently embarrassed. 'I was dismissed,' she said in a low voice. 'Signora Heather was very angry with me.'

'But why? Surely you can't have done anything so very terrible?'

'I said something—I had no right—I didn't mean any harm, but nobody is allowed to speak of it in that house—because of you.'

'Because of me? I don't understand. Why should I care what anyone says?'

'Please, Signorina, I don't want to get into any more trouble.'

'I won't make trouble for you,' Helen said gently. 'But I think you should tell me what happened.'

'But you will be angry with me too,' Sara wailed, 'if they haven't told you—'

'I won't be angry,' Helen insisted.

After a little more carefully calculated fencing Sara allowed herself to be 'persuaded'.

'It was about Signor Lorenzo,' she whispered, 'because he was supposed to marry her—and then he didn't—'

'What do you mean?' Helen asked, frowning. 'Who was he supposed to marry?'

'Signora Heather. She came out to Sicily last year to marry him, but on their wedding day he vanished. She went to the cathedral, but he'd gone. He left her a letter saying he couldn't marry her.'

'Don't be silly. If that had happened, I'd have heard.'

'They won't have it mentioned,' Sara said. 'It's a great scandal and nobody must speak of it.'

'You said "the cathedral",' Angie echoed, in a daze. 'Do you mean—?'

'Palermo cathedral. It was a very grand affair. All the family had come from far and wide, and the building was full. There was a great choir and a beautiful bride—but no bridegroom. He'd abandoned her.'

Sara spoke the last words with relish, but Helen was past noticing. The world seemed to be fragmenting about her, and reforming itself into a monstrous shape.

'But—Heather married Renato last year,' she murmured. 'Surely—?'

'Of course. Signora Baptista arranged it.'

'Arranged—?'

'It had to be done for the family's honour. The wedding was barely two months after Signor Lorenzo left her standing at the altar. She had to save her pride, so she married his brother, but she was still weeping for him. Perhaps even now—oh, forgive me! I've said too much.'

'No,' Helen said, speaking like someone in a dream. 'You haven't said too much.'

Sara touched her hand. 'You didn't know?'

'No,' Helen whispered. 'I didn't know.' She pulled herself together. 'But it's all in the past. It doesn't affect me.'

'Of course not. And surely Signor Lorenzo has forgotten her and loves only you—it's just that—'

'Go on,' Helen said in a dead voice.

'They say Signor Renato is very angry and jealous because his wife and his brother are still so fond of each other. Last year—'

She shouldn't listen to this gossip but she couldn't help herself. The poison had crept into her ear and there was no escaping it now.

'What happened last year?' she whispered.

'Signor Lorenzo went to England, but the next day I was in her room when the phone rang. She answered it and said, "Lorenzo", then she ordered me out. As I left the room I heard her say, "It's all right, I'm alone." Then later she told me she was going away. She didn't say where but—well—I heard through the door—'

'Go on.'

'She told him that she would be with him that night,' Sara said in a low voice.

'I don't believe it,' Helen said firmly. 'You must have misheard.'

If she had to listen to any more she knew she would go mad. Forcing a smile to her face she got to her feet, managed to say goodbye, and fled.

Left alone, Sara finished all the cakes and drank the coffee, relishing every crumb, every last drop. She had fantasised how she would hit back at Heather for her dismissal, but who would have thought the chance would present itself so opportunely? It had been a good day's work.

* * *

Somehow Helen got herself to the villa that was to be her future home, and where she wouldn't be disturbed. Her head was spinning and she needed time to come to terms with what she'd heard.

Lorenzo and Heather had been in love, had planned to marry.

And he'd left her at the altar.

Perhaps it wasn't true. Why had she believed Sara so easily? It might all be an invention.

Yet a memory disturbed her; Heather, showing her to her room on the first day, saying, 'It's where Angie and I slept when I came out here—' Then the sudden awkward silence.

She'd asked, 'Did Renato meet you at the airport?' Taking it for granted that Renato had been the bridegroom.

But the bridegroom had been Lorenzo. And Heather had swiftly changed the subject, embarrassed to realise that Helen didn't know the truth.

Because Lorenzo hadn't told her. That was the worst thing of all.

She'd thought they were close, lovers and best friends. That was the strength of their relationship, that it was built on friendship as well as passion. And friendship meant trust and confidence. Suddenly all trust was blown away.

There had been the suggestion that Heather had never stopped loving Lorenzo, marrying Renato on the rebound, and the unsubtle hint that Lorenzo had regretted his action and continued to pine for the woman who was now his sister-in-law: that together they had betrayed her husband.

Heather and Lorenzo were there in her mind, their heads close, laughing together. How readily she put her arms about him, how eagerly he embraced her back.

It was nonsense, she told herself firmly. They hugged as brother and sister, under Renato's eyes. But only under his eyes? The question slid into her mind like a snake.

And when Heather lay in the hospital, her life in danger, Lorenzo had wept. Renato, that hard man, had looked like a stone. But Lorenzo had wept.

It meant nothing. Renato closed up, told his feelings to nobody. It was his way. Lorenzo's emotions were near the surface, and he could talk about things.

But he hadn't told his intended bride that he'd jilted another bride at the altar.

That was the fact she couldn't escape. It stood across her path like a monolith, barring her way to her wedding.

CHAPTER NINE

SHE tried twice to call Lorenzo in France, but both times the calls were interrupted, and she realised that this was hopeless. The talk they must have couldn't be conducted over the telephone.

The time before he returned was terrible. Everything she saw seemed lit up by a livid light. Heather's smile, once so sweet and friendly, now seemed to have a jeering, cynical twist. And wherever she looked she saw cruel concealment, knowledge hidden from her because she was nothing.

If she hoped that Lorenzo's return would provide a chance to talk she was soon disillusioned.

'*Cara*, I want to be alone with you too,' he said, swiftly kissing her as they sat in the back of the chauffeur driven car from the airport. 'But Renato's going to keep me at it until the last minute. And when I'm not working I'm entertaining. But it's all in a good cause, so that after the wedding we can enjoy our honeymoon.'

'Darling, please,' she begged, her eyes on the chauffeur's back. 'It's important.'

For answer he took her into his arms and kissed her hard. 'That is important,' he said. 'Loving each other is important.'

He was at his most charming as he said it, but suddenly his charm seemed almost frightening. It was such a potent weapon. Was there something a little ruthless about the way he used it? She searched his face, trying to see there the man who could jilt a woman at the altar and take her to bed when she was his brother's wife. But all she could see was his charm.

Then it was the day for her family to arrive, filling the Residenza's guest rooms, plus half the nearby hotels. Her parents were beside themselves with joy as Baptista showed them over the splendid house of which they'd heard so much. They basked in the honour shown them by this great lady, and Helen wondered how they would feel if they knew that she was desperately thinking of calling the wedding off.

But that was overreacting, she assured herself. Somehow she would have a long talk with Lorenzo and he would explain everything. Of course he hadn't betrayed Renato with his wife. Sara's story had been garbled. As for his behaviour in the cathedral—there must be an explanation. He would tell her, and everything would be all right.

But the days were rushing by in a blur of parties and shopping trips, and suddenly it was the last night, and Lorenzo was being swept off in a tidal wave of male relations, for a final carouse.

'Darling, please—' she tried to plead, but Renato intervened.

'Don't worry, Elena. We won't let him get too drunk, and we'll bring him home safely.'

He was as good as his word. At two in the morning he and Bernardo helped their brother up the stairs, reasonably sober, considering it had been a stag night, but way past talking coherently. Helen watched their progress in despair.

That night she lay awake, wretched, trying to picture the future, seeing only a blank. She dropped into an uneasy doze at six o'clock, and was awoken an hour later by the maid with her coffee. Now the day had to be faced.

Her bedroom was crowded with women all eager to help her on with her bridal gown, made of satin that had been specially woven for extra weight, draped over a wide, crinolined skirt. It wasn't white, but ivory, a better colour for Helen's black hair and warm skin. The skirt was heavily embroidered, with tiny sparkling jewels sewn into rosettes, and a diamond tiara to hold the veil in place. It was a romantic dream of a dress, but now its very magnificence filled her with anguish.

'Where's Lorenzo?' she said urgently. 'I must talk to Lorenzo.'

There was a united scream from every woman in the room.

'You can't see the bridegroom before the wedding,' her mother said firmly. 'It's unlucky.'

'Oh, Mamma, that's just superstition.'

There was a knock at the door and her father's voice called, 'Are you all ready?' The next moment he was in the room, laughing and bawling his enjoyment.

'She wants to see Lorenzo,' Mamma complained.

'She can't do that,' he roared.

'Poppa, I must—'

'Nonsense,' he said, standing in front of the door, twice her size, daring her to try to remove him. 'This is just female foolishness. I won't listen.'

'But perhaps we should,' her mother suggested worriedly. She had seen something in her daughter's face that made her contradict him for once.

'No,' Nicolo said forcefully. 'Trust me, Mamma, I know what's best.'

And Mamma subsided, to Helen's burning resentment. Poppa was still standing in front of the door, implacable, confident of his own rightness in everything. She turned and stormed out onto the terrace.

The cars were moving off. Helen watched them stream away down the hill, knowing that Lorenzo would be in one of them, with all the others filled with relatives. The first car grew fainter and fainter until it vanished out of sight.

Her father appeared behind her, putting his hands on her shoulders.

'Now it's our turn,' he said kindly. 'And I'm the proudest Poppa in the world.'

Good-tempered now that his will had prevailed, he offered her his arm with an air of old world gallantry. Helen took it, and they went out together.

But as she descended the grand stairway another bride seemed to be there with her; Heather, in bridal glory, very like her own, beginning the same journey to the same cathedral to marry the same man. Only he hadn't been there, and the bride had been humiliated, and had to return home, broken hearted, to face the world's scorn. How could anyone do a thing so devastating, so wicked and cruel?

In no time at all it seemed that they had passed through the countryside, had reached the city and were driving down the Corso Vittorio Emanuele, the long, straight road that led to the piazza, and the entrance to the cathedral.

With an air of pride Poppa handed her out of the car, and the procession began.

The cathedral seemed to stretch away into infinity. As she began the long journey down the great aisle she had the strange sensation that the altar was retreating and she would be here forever, striving to move forward and getting nowhere.

Lorenzo was there, looking down the aisle towards her, smiling as she neared. It was going to be all right, she thought as she saw the love blazing from him. How could she doubt him when he looked at her like that? He even reached out his hand as she neared, so great was his eagerness, and a murmur of approval ran around the congregation. Such an ardent groom. Such a lucky bride.

The service washed over her, until the moment she heard Lorenzo say,

'I, Lorenzo Luigi, take thee, Elena, to be my lawfully wedded wife. I promise to be true to you in good times and in bad, in sickness and in health till death us do part.'

Then it was her turn. Her hand was in his. He was looking at her, his eyes warm with love, a gentle, expectant smile on his lips. In a dream she began to say,

'I, Elena, take thee, Lorenzo—'

It was as though a hand clamped over her throat, choking off the words. She tried again. 'I, Elena—'

The silence seemed to stretch forever, filled with Lorenzo's surprise, the soft buzz as the congregation sensed something wrong, 'till death us do part' tolling like bells in her head, her own heartbeat growing louder because she was horrified by what she was about to do.

But she had no choice.

'I'm sorry,' she whispered. 'I can't—'

Lorenzo gave her his delightful smile. 'It's all right, *carissima*. One short step and we'll be together forever.'

Forever. With a man she couldn't trust.

'No,' she cried. 'I'm sorry, I can't. *I can't!*'

She had a brief glimpse of his face as her words registered, then she darted away fast enough to evade his restraining hand, running away from Lorenzo, running as if her life depended on it.

The cathedral was a blur about her as she sped down the long aisle. She was vaguely aware of shocked faces, but they were gone the next instant. Then she was out in the piazza, running towards the parked cars. She threw herself into the front one, gasping, *'Drive!'*

After a brief look at her distraught face the chauffeur started up. They were speeding away as Lorenzo rushed out of the church, looking madly around him.

'*Elena! ELENA!*'

'No,' she wept, crouching down in the back seat, her hands over her ears. 'I'm not Elena,' she muttered. 'I'm Helen. *Helen!* You never understood—never—'

They would be following her soon. If only she could get home and throw off the wedding dress that belonged to a stranger called Elena. Without it she could escape from this place, be herself again, and forget that she'd ever been deceived by a sweet-talking charmer called Lorenzo Martelli.

As they headed for the Residenza she pulled herself up onto the seat and looked through the rear window. Another car was in pursuit, gaining on them.

'Faster,' she urged the driver.

In a few minutes they were swinging into the courtyard and she was fleeing up the stairs to her room. She slammed the door shut and stood clinging to it, breathless, overwhelmed by what she had done.

She heard his footsteps running up the stairs, coming towards her.

'Elena—what happened? For pity's sake tell me.'

'Later,' she choked. 'I need a moment—'

Silence. Then his footsteps walking away. Her relief was short-lived. A moment later she heard him coming along the terrace, and hurriedly locked the great window. His shadow appeared and the lock rattled.

'Open this or I'll break the glass,' he said harshly.

She had no doubt that he meant it. She turned the key and backed away. She was trembling.

Lorenzo was as she'd never seen him before. His face was hard, but after that brief outburst he was in command of himself.

'What happened?' he asked quietly. 'Did you lose your nerve?'

'No, I lost my love,' she said, very pale.
'What?'

'I don't know you any more, Lorenzo. And if I don't know you, how can I love you?'

'What are you talking about?' he whispered. *'Who are you?'*

'You know who I am. I'm the man who loves you.'

'No, I thought I knew that man, but suddenly there's a new one in his place. He does terrible things and hides them behind a smiling face, and lies to the woman who loves him because she doesn't really matter. What else are you capable of that I don't dream of?'

'I don't understand a word you're saying.'

'I *know*,' she said fiercely. 'I know about you and Heather.'

'There is no me and Heather.'

'But there was. You were going to be married, weren't you? And you stood her up at the altar.'

'So you did the same to me!' he shouted. 'What were you trying to do? Get even on behalf of all women?'

'It's nothing like that. You suddenly looked different. I tried to talk to you about it but you could never spare me the time.'

'Only because everything was so rushed for the wedding.'

'You should have told me long ago.'

'Like when? On the first day when you turned me down before we'd been introduced?

Faithless and unreliable. Remember saying
that? I was likely to tell you then, wasn't I?'

'Yes, it would have been too much confir-
mation.'

'It didn't matter then, can't you see? We
were just friends, laughing all the time. And
lately—I suppose I didn't think. All right, I
was thoughtless, but I love you. Isn't that
enough?'

'No, it's not enough,' she said wildly. 'You
treated me with contempt.'

'That's not true.'

'Oh, you don't think it's treating me with
contempt to conceal from me something that
everyone else knew, letting them laugh at me,
pity me, counting on me not finding out until
too late? No, of course you don't. Because
that's how a Sicilian man behaves, isn't it?'

'Will you stop talking like that?' he roared.
'All that prejudice of yours is damned silly.'

'No, it isn't, it's true. I thought you were
different, but you're not. And my prejudices,
as you call them, are based on reality. The little
woman is entitled to know exactly what *he*
tells her and no more. If even you can behave
like that, I was right all the time.'

'All right, I should have told you, but it's so far in the past—'

'Little more than a year ago.'

'It's still over.'

He was a creature of the moment, she realised with despair. What was over was over, whether it was one year or ten.

'Heather and I weren't right for each other—' he began to say.

'You must have loved her once or it would never have got as far as a wedding.'

Lorenzo tore his hair. Analysing people, especially himself, came hard to him, and the effort was doing his head in. But he tried his best. 'I thought I did,' he said. 'I was wrong.'

'Oh, you changed your mind just like that, and left her standing there to be laughed at.'

'That wedding was a terrible mistake. Heather and I didn't love each other.'

'Didn't you? Are you sure you didn't regret it afterwards? She was very convinced you two still had a yen for each other, maybe still do—'

'She? Who?'

'Sara. She was a maid here when it happened. And later, she took the call when

Heather dashed to England to be with you, although she was married to Renato by then—'

'Sara? *Mio Dio!*' He threw up his hands. 'So that's it. Heather dismissed her for stealing. She must have had a wonderful time getting her revenge.'

'You mean it's not true? You didn't leave Heather at the altar?'

'Yes, I did, and I'm ashamed of it, but if you'd just let me explain—'

'It's too late for that. You should have told me earlier, and not left me to find out from someone else. What were you thinking of?'

'I was thinking of you,' he said simply. 'Just you. You drove everything else out of my head. Maybe I should have remembered the past and realised, but—' he shrugged '—I suppose I just assumed that our love was so special that it could overcome everything.'

She turned away swiftly, not to let him see that this affected her. It was less his words than his tone, suddenly gentle and almost bewildered, that touched her heart. But she fought the tears back. He'd always known how to make her weaken, but she couldn't afford to weaken now.

Lorenzo took hold of her, drawing her close although her head was still averted from him.

'Listen to me, darling, I was wrong. I'm sorry, but I love you more than anything in the world. It's not too late. If we go back to the cathedral now, we can still be married. People will think it strange, but let them. If we love each other—'

'Stop it, stop it!' she cried, wrenching herself free. 'I can't simply turn the clock back like that. You talk about love, but what is your love worth? How long does it last? You changed your mind about Heather. What about when you change your mind about me, Lorenzo? It's not so easy after the wedding, but I'm sure you'd have found a way to do as you pleased.'

His face had been pale before, but at this it became a greyish colour, as though he were dying. 'Be careful what you say,' he whispered.

'Why? Should I be afraid of you?'

'No, I think perhaps you should be afraid of *you*. You're on the verge of saying things that will make it impossible for us ever to find our way back to each other.'

'There *is* no way back. I made a mistake. Luckily I saw it in time.'

He put his hand over her mouth. 'Hush. Don't talk like that, Elena. For pity's sake, leave us some hope.'

'Don't call me Elena. She's someone else, someone you can manipulate because she's stupid. And I *have* been stupid, haven't I? Everything about our marriage suddenly fell into place so neatly—*too* neatly. It was always obvious but I wouldn't see it.'

'What do you mean?'

'Look me in the eye and tell me you had nothing to do with me getting that job at the hotel.'

'What on earth—?'

'Tell me.'

He took a deep breath. 'I called Erik and suggested you were ideal to work there, but you *are*. Axel Roderick wouldn't have given you the job otherwise.'

'But you did call him and fix me up with a job in Sicily—to suit yourself?'

He stared. 'If you want to put it like that. I just thought I was taking care of the problems.

I knew you still wanted your career, and this way you could still have it and marry me.'

'You manipulated it,' she repeated. 'You wanted me, so you pulled all the right strings.'

'Yes, I wanted you,' he shouted. 'I'd have done anything to get you to marry me. You make it sound like a crime.'

'I just wonder what would have happened when it suited you to make me leave my job and stay at home all day. More string-pulling, and suddenly I wouldn't have a choice.'

'You really believe that I'd do that to you?' he asked, aghast.

'I don't know. I told you, I don't know *you* any more. All I know is that I walked right into something I always promised myself I'd avoid. There are too many unanswered questions. You say Sara was being spiteful, but it's true about you and Heather. You *are* very close. I've seen it, but I thought it was just brother and sister—'

'So it is! What the hell are you suggesting. That Heather and I—?'

'What happened when you went to England and sent for her to join you, and she promised to be with you *that night*?'

There was a long silence. As it stretched on and on she knew that she'd made a dreadful mistake. Lorenzo looked like a man who'd received a mortal blow. Before her eyes he grew older, wearier. It was there in his face that he'd given up on something. Given up on her? On hope? On love?

'If you've been thinking that of me,' he said at last, 'then I'm surprised you got as far as the altar.'

'I kept hoping to talk to you—that we might clear it up—'

'Talk? Between me and the woman who thinks I slept with my brother's wife? How you must have despised me all this time. What is there to talk about?' He gave a mirthless laugh. 'What could we say to each other, you and I?'

'Nothing,' she said dully.

He stared at her in a kind of horror. 'You never understood how much I loved you. It happened right from the start but I wouldn't face it because I knew you didn't want me. All that friendship talk was just a cover for the fact that I was off my head about you. I thought about you non-stop. I thought about you when I should have been working.

'I nearly went crazy when I had to leave New York. I was jealous as hell of Erik. I kept wanting to beg you not to marry him because you belonged to me. Yes, *belonged* to me. Mine. Nobody else's. I'm a Sicilian, and that's how we think. Sorry about that, but it's true. It's not modern, not liberated. It's Sicilian. If you marry me, you *belong* to me. But what you never thought of was that *I* belonged to *you*. In my heart and mind I was yours, your property to do as you liked with. I'd have done anything you asked, anything at all. I'd have lain down and invited you to walk over me if it made you happy. And, be honest, Helen, that's a damned sight more than you could ever say.'

She stared at him, stricken. It was true.

Lorenzo spoke his next words with a bitterness that she could never have imagined from him. 'I loved you more than I've ever loved anyone, or ever will again. But now—I think it would have been better if we'd never met.'

She became aware of a rumbling noise growing louder. Cars had begun to arrive, doors banged, footsteps thundered and suddenly a vast crowd flooded into the room from the terrace.

'*Disgraciatu! Disgraciatu!*' The cry filled the room and Helen was never sure who'd uttered the words. Her father, perhaps, bearing down on her in a towering rage.

'My daughter!' he shouted. 'That my daughter should do this! And with the whole city looking on.'

'Poppa, I'm sorry it happened that way—' she tried to say.

'You've brought shame on your family,' he screamed. 'You've dishonoured your promise, dishonoured your father—'

'Wait.' Lorenzo laid a hand on Poppa's arm and he immediately tried to be calmer.

'I offer my apologies to the Martelli family,' he choked. 'I am shamed to the dust.'

A look of disgust passed across Lorenzo's face. 'Nothing that has happened today has shamed anybody,' he said firmly. 'Elena changed her mind, as she had the right to do. In time, we will both be glad that she had the courage.'

Helen was standing by the bed, holding onto one of the posts, feeling as though all the strength had drained out of her after the anguish of the last few days. But at the realisation that Lorenzo was going to defend her she fixed her eyes on him.

It wasn't totally a surprise. She had always known that he was generous. But for him to stand up for her now, when he was lacerated by humiliation, brought tears to her eyes.

But her father was still in full flow.

'You are kinder than she deserves,' he cried. 'But to leave you at the altar—there can be no forgiveness for such a cowardly, disgraceful act.'

'I hope you are wrong,' Lorenzo said, very pale. 'Because I myself once committed just such an act. A year ago I walked out on my wedding, in the same cathedral.'

Poppa blenched as he realised that Lorenzo could construe his words as an insult to himself. 'That is quite different—' he hurried to say.

'It is not different at all,' Lorenzo said firmly. 'I was granted forgiveness, and I am the last person who should blame Elena. Nor will I allow anyone else to blame her. She had her reasons—' he took a choking breath '—good reasons. The blame is mine.'

That silenced them for a moment, but then Giorgio shouldered his way to the front. Either he hadn't heard Lorenzo's words, or he was too full of rage and disappointment to take them in.

'You fool!' he screamed at Helen. 'You had your chance—a chance for all of us—and you threw it away.'

'Be silent!' Lorenzo warned him.

Giorgio ignored him. 'You think only of yourself,' he bawled at Helen. 'You get some stupid idea in your head and your whole family has to suffer. Shame on you.'

'That's enough!'

At first nobody recognised that the fierce command had come from Lorenzo, so unlike himself did he sound. Gradually the room grew quiet, and they all turned to see a stern faced man where a boy had once been.

'I forbid you to say another word,' Lorenzo said, speaking slowly and emphatically for Giorgio's benefit. 'You have nothing to say to Elena Angolini. Not a thing. She hasn't harmed you, and I shall not allow you to harm her.'

'*You* will not—?' Giorgio scoffed.

'*I* will not allow,' Lorenzo repeated coldly.

Giorgio cast him a belligerent look which made Renato and Bernardo start forward, but Lorenzo halted them with a gesture. They stepped back. They had seen something in their brother that had never been there before and their faces expressed their satisfaction.

'Get out of Sicily,' Lorenzo said.

'Who are you to—?'

'Get out now, on the afternoon plane. A car will take you to the airport. Collect your passport and leave this minute. If you don't, bad things will happen to you.'

Nobody had ever seen Lorenzo like this before. Giorgio made one last effort at assertion, but it amounted to no more than taking a deep breath, and collapsed at once. He began to inch backwards through the crowd that parted for him, until he turned and ran. His wife slipped out after him, and the others began to drift away too.

When only the Martellis were left Lorenzo turned to his family.

'I would like to speak to Elena alone, please.'

They obeyed at once. None of them would have defied the commanding man who stood there. Only Baptista hesitated, stepping up to Helen and kissing her cheek. She looked at her son, who responded with a brief smile and said almost inaudibly, 'Thank you, Mamma. Now, please go. And send us some coffee and sandwiches.'

'I don't need anything,' Helen said.

'Yes, you do,' he told her firmly. 'You need strong black coffee, and then you'll have something to eat.'

It was a voice she had never heard from him before. She stared at him.

CHAPTER TEN

WHEN Fede had led Baptista from the room Lorenzo took hold of Helen's arms and moved her until he could push her gently down to sit on the bed.

'Helen, I want you to listen to me very seriously,' he said, still speaking in the new tone, as though it wasn't really Lorenzo, but some older, more serious man who had taken his place. 'Somehow we have to deal with this mess.'

'We? It's my mess. I'll sort it.'

'You can't. Not alone. We have to present a united front.'

Her laugh had a touch of hysteria. 'What did you do last time? No, I'm sorry, I shouldn't have said that.'

'It's a fair question. I vanished for several days. Your way is more courageous.'

'Sure, I'm a real heroine, aren't I?' she said bitterly.

'Yes, you are. With all that pressure from your family and mine, with me so determined to marry you at all costs that I never gave you time to think—you found the guts to say no to the lot of us. Good for you, although—' his mockery was directed at himself, 'I can't say I'm feeling great about it right now.'

'You're actually defending me?'

'What should I do? Rail about how shocking it is to leave someone at the altar? *Me?*'

'But you're a man. Remember telling me that a woman just couldn't do such a thing in Sicily?'

'That was long ago, and we were making jokes. I said many things—ah, Helen, the things I said!' He voice shook suddenly and he moved away so that she couldn't see his face.

His pain was almost tangible. She wanted to reach out to him, but she'd shut herself off from that, forever.

There was a knock on the door. She darted to the window, not wanting to be seen by the servant who'd brought the tray, and went out onto the terrace. From here she could see the courtyard where there were still several cars, and suddenly Giorgio and his wife emerged.

After a moment Lorenzo came to fetch her. He too stood watching Giorgio's departure, until the man himself became aware of them, regarding him from above. An ugly grin split his face, and he raised both hands until the back of his knuckles were against his forehead, the index fingers pointing upwards, so that the effect was of a pair of horns. Then he dashed for the car.

Horns. The sign of the cuckold.

'Did he mean—?' Helen began, incensed.

Lorenzo shrugged. 'He's an ignorant man. Forget him.'

He led her back inside. 'Perhaps you should change?' he suggested.

Most of her clothes were packed up in suit-cases, ready for the honeymoon, but she found a pair of jeans and a sweater and took them into the bathroom. When she emerged Lorenzo had poured her a coffee and set out some sand-wiches. She recalled her mother, whose solu-tion to all problems was food, and realised, with a sense of shock, that Lorenzo was caring for her in the same way.

She took some of the sandwiches he pressed on her, and drank the black coffee, heavily sweetened, because somehow this new Lorenzo understood that she was in a state of shock even greater than his own.

'Aren't you having some too?' she asked.

'No, I don't need it.'

He would get drunk later.

She wondered what was happening downstairs where a multitude of guests must be fed and, more difficult, given some sort of explanation. The enormity of what she'd done suddenly hit her like a hammer.

'Oh, my God!' she said, sitting down on the bed suddenly.

'What is it?' He sat beside her.

'All those people down there—all that food—the wedding cake—'

'Don't worry,' he said lightly. 'We've done this before.'

'How can you make a joke of it?'

'It's better than weeping.' But then the attempted humour fell from his face, and she caught a glimpse of the reality, an emotional man hurt to the heart and near breaking point.

'How would you like me to act, Helen? Like your version of a Sicilian male, wield a knife, threaten blood vengeance on you and your family to the third generation? That's what we do, isn't it?' A bitter mockery of her and her prejudices underlay the calm tone. 'And you know what?' he went on wryly, 'Part of me would like to do all those things. But it's not my style, and I don't think I could carry it off.'

If only she could comfort his pain, but she'd forfeited that right forever. She could do nothing but watch him suffer.

'So,' he said at last, 'what are we going to do?'

'The sooner I leave Sicily the better.'

'No. The more I think about it, the more it seems to me that you mustn't return to New York.'

'I can't stay here.'

'That's exactly what you ought to do. Why should you run away as though you'd done something wrong, when we both know that you haven't?' He'd fixed his gaze at somewhere just over her left shoulder. 'If you go back, can you imagine what your life will be like—your mother and father, that great oaf, making your life a misery?'

'I shall have my job.'

'Of sorts. Elroys won't be pleased at you running out on the task they've given you here. You'll be relegated to the backwaters. Stay at this job for a couple of years, make a success of it, then go back in triumph. But if you return now—it makes my blood run cold to think of you exposed to Giorgio's vindictiveness when I'm not there to—' He broke off.

'To protect me? Say it.'

'It doesn't matter. You know I'm right. I made things go wrong for you. Let me help to put them straight again. You needn't be afraid of my troubling you. All that is at an end between us. But there can still be a kind of friendship.'

'After this?'

'Why not? Heather and I became brother and sister. You and I had a good friendship. We should have treasured it for what it was, and not tried to overload it. Let me help you. Please, Helen.'

He was right. The thought of going home wasn't pleasant, but it had never occurred to her that she could remain here. Whichever way she looked the future seemed to be a blank.

'If only I knew what to do,' she said desperately.

'But *I* know. You should heed your friend's advice.' He took her hands between his and she felt the warmth and strength from him flowing into her.

'I'll drive you to Palermo now,' he said, 'and you can move into the hotel. We'll leave here by the back way so that you won't have to see anyone. Just take an overnight bag and I'll send your luggage on later. Leave all the explaining to me. And don't worry. Everything is going to be all right.'

Helen's office in the Elroy-Palermo was spacious, richly furnished with antiques, and only slightly less grandiose than Axel Roderick's. From the start she had a lot of power since he'd recognised her flair and was eager for her to use it, as long as he looked good.

The renovations were proceeding fast and it would soon be time for the grand opening. She was working an eighteen-hour day now, thankful that she had her own room in the hotel, and even more thankful that work left her no time to think.

'By the way,' Axel said to her one morning, 'it seems that your Martelli connections are going to benefit us, even if you didn't marry one of them. Well done for putting the company first.'

'Sorry?'

'Didn't you negotiate the Martelli contract?'

'I don't interfere with the running of individual departments.'

'Sure, sure, that's the story. But why are they giving us rock bottom prices *and* their very best produce if not for you, eh? Well done! Keep it up.'

He was convinced and there was no persuading him otherwise. And, since Helen could hardly complain to Martellis that their prices were too low, she was forced to accept the situation.

Nobody could get to see her without an appointment, but she made an exception when her secretary announced that Signora Heather Martelli had arrived. It was two months since the aborted wedding and the first time she'd spoken to Heather since, and she wondered

what they could possibly say. But Heather had
brought her baby, and in exclaiming over him
the ice was broken.

'Did you hear about Angie's baby?' Heather
asked as Angie cradled little Vittorio.

'Yes, it was in the newspaper. Is Bernardo
disappointed that it's a girl?'

'You must be kidding. He's over the moon.
His little *piccina* has only to gurgle and he
turns to jelly.'

'*Bernardo?*'

Heather chuckled. 'Yes, even Bernardo. It's
amazing what happiness can do to a man. You
should see my Renato, always sneaking a few
minutes off work to come and ''see that
Vittorio is all right''. And when he and
Bernardo get together they swap baby stories.
It's helped to bring Bernardo into the heart of
the family. He's even going to take the
Martelli name. That makes Baptista so happy.'

She paused a moment before adding,
'Something else made her happy too, that letter
you wrote her.'

'I had to write after slipping out like that
without seeing her—I shouldn't have done
it—'

'No, Lorenzo explained that he'd persuaded you, and Baptista said he was right. She was glad when I told her I was coming to visit you. We've worried about you, stranded alone here. We hoped you'd come back to see us.'

'How could I—after everything—?'

'You needn't worry about Lorenzo. He's in Spain.'

Helen found something to do on her desk. 'How is he?'

'Making a big success. He's a great sales-man.'

Helen nodded. 'Yes, once he gets talking he can sell anything to anybody,' she murmured wryly.

'But sometimes he leaves important things out,' Heather said. Her eyes were gentle.

Helen nodded, uncertain how much it would be wise to say.

'He told me why you broke it off. If only he'd explained everything to you long ago this could all have been avoided. Helen, you must believe me, Lorenzo and I were never really in love. We fancied we were for a time, but we'd never have got engaged if Renato hadn't pushed us into it. One of them had to marry and provide a Martelli heir, and he didn't want to bother. So, having met me and looked me over, he decided that I was suitable, and more or less ordered Lorenzo to propose.'

'And he *did*?'

'Lorenzo was different in those days. More of a boy, not the man he's become now. He looked up to Renato as the head of the family, and, as I say, we were briefly infatuated; enough to think it might work. So I came here to marry him, but then Renato and I fell in love.

'But what could we do? The wedding was only a few days away. How could we tell Lorenzo? Luckily he sensed the truth, and had the courage to walk out of the cathedral and save us all from disaster. It was terrible at the time, but Renato and I will be grateful to him all our lives for leaving us free to marry.'

'But—' Helen couldn't go on.

'You heard Sara's version, highly coloured for revenge. What else did she say?'

'That Baptista arranged your marriage.'

'Oh, she did. Renato and I were left floundering, at odds with each other, not knowing what to say. We might still be floundering if she hadn't found a way to settle things, but it was a love match for all that.'

'You weren't pining for Lorenzo?'

'Not for a moment.'

Helen said the next words with difficulty. 'When Lorenzo went to England and called you—Sara said you promised to be with him that night.'

'I had to. He called me in a panic to say he'd been arrested, and I promised to be there by evening to bail him out. But when I got there they wouldn't let him out in case he left the country, so he had to sleep in the cell.'

'But why was he arrested?'

'He was driving a fraction over the limit, and when a policeman stopped him he took a swing at him. Actually he barely touched him. Even the policeman admitted that in court next morning. And there was no accident, nobody hurt. The magistrate fined him and told him not to be such an idiot another time. Then we fled the country as fast as we could, and were back here later that day. I'm sure Sara made it sound like a lovers' assignation, but actually it was that incident that really made us brother and sister. Lorenzo says I nagged him all the way home, without pausing for breath.'

'Oh, heavens!' Helen buried her face in her hands. 'I've been such a fool.'

'No, Lorenzo has been a fool. He should have told you everything, but that's his way— put it off and hope for the best. At least, that's how he used to be. These days I'm not so sure.'

'You two always seemed so close—'

'We are close. I love him dearly—as a brother. And there's a special bond between people who have nearly married and then didn't.'

Helen's smile was sad. She had neither seen nor heard from Lorenzo since that day. He had taken her to the hotel, bid her a courteous goodbye, and driven off. The next morning her bags were delivered. Since then, silence. Well, what else had she expected?

The year was closing in, but Palermo remained a pleasant place where it was possible to eat at the pavement cafés even in December. Helen decided to remain where she was for Christmas and immure herself in her hotel apartment, concentrating on a thousand problems, including the big one that still plagued her—how to get huge publicity for the hotel's February opening.

The management back in New York had insisted on this unlikely date so that the name of the Elroy Palermo could establish itself before the summer. They were expecting Axel Roderick to open with something spectacular, but so far he hadn't thought of the crucial idea. Nor had she, and time was pressing.

Sometimes, late at night, she would close her office and stroll across to her two room apartment. She would listen to her own footsteps in the darkened building, and consider how far she had come since that day, nearly a year ago, when she had returned from Boston to New York, eager to complete her training and become a successful businesswoman.

She'd done it. She had power, authority, and a large salary. Her word was listened to with respect and no family demands tied her down. She had everything she'd always wanted.

But she was alone.

Her ambitions had never included that, because she couldn't have anticipated meeting the man who'd combined love and laughter and left an impression on her heart that she couldn't erase. From her apartment window she could just make out the lights of Mondello harbour, where the Santa Maria lay. And Lorenzo's words seemed to echo about her.

'—what you never thought of was that *I* belonged to *you*—I loved you more than I've ever loved anyone, or ever will again—better if we had never met— All that is at an end between us—'

He'd offered her friendship, but friendship could never be enough. She knew, now it was too late, that she loved him more than life. She wanted to belong to him in the equal compact of belonging that he'd spoken of. But he no longer wanted her.

All that is at an end between us.

One afternoon when the chatter of voices grew too much for her, she slipped out of the hotel for some fresh air and went walking down by the harbour. She didn't mean to head for the *Santa Maria*, but somehow her feet found their way there, and stopped so that she could look wistfully at the bobbing single tall mast.

'Helen, how good to see you?'

She looked around to see Bernardo, smiling.

'How are you?' she asked politely.

'Better than ever in my life before.'

'Congratulations on your baby.'

'You haven't seen her yet, have you? That's terrible. Come with me to Montedoro now.'

'Oh, I don't think—'

'Of course you must. I'll drive you back afterwards.'

He was steering her towards his car, his hand tucked firmly under her arm. It would be pleasant to see Angie, whom she'd always liked.

As they climbed the mildness of the coastal climate fell away, and when Montedoro appeared just up ahead, its roofs were white with a light dusting of snow. Soon they had reached the beautiful old house with its courtyard and fountain, where Bernardo had been born and spent the first twelve years of his life. As they made their way through the courtyard Angie's face appeared at the window.

'I've brought someone to see you,' Bernardo said, kissing his wife.

Angie embraced her warmly and Helen said, 'I'm longing to see your little baby.'

'She's just through there,' Angie said, pointing behind. 'But Helen—'

'What? Did I come at a bad time?'

Angie seemed to make a decision. 'No, you came at a perfect time. Just go through.'

She pointed the way to the comfortable main room, and Helen went ahead. But on the threshold she stopped.

'Hello,' Lorenzo said.

He was sitting by the fire, the baby in his arms. In the split second before he looked up Helen took in the whole picture, the unselfconscious way he held the child, smiling into her face. It flashed across her mind that she'd never seen anything so delightful.

Then his face seemed to close against her. His smile faded, replaced by a polite formality that shut her out.

'Hello,' he said again.

'I—thought you were in Spain.'

'I got back yesterday. I had to come and visit my niece.'

'I met Bernardo and he insisted on bringing me to see Helen and the baby.'

A touch of warmth returned to his face. 'She's a charmer. Come and see.'

He indicated the place on the sofa beside her and when she'd sat down he gently placed the infant in her lap.

'How are you with babies?' he said.

'You ask me that? With all the relations I've got?'

'Me, too. I've been practising for years.'

They exchanged cautious smiles.

'What's her name?' Helen asked.

'It's still under discussion. She'll have several names, Anna, Baptista, Lenora and Marta. But which one will come first will probably be argued about until the day of the baptism.'

Angie bustled in with coffee and cakes. Lorenzo declined, having already eaten, and took the baby back into his arms. He had none of the awkwardness so many young men showed with babies. His pleasure in her was genuine.

He was thinner, and there was a new tension about him, as though he'd lived the last few weeks on hot coals. Lorenzo, whose nature was so carefree, now looked as though care was a constant companion.

My doing, she thought sadly. *He said it would have been better if we'd never met, and it would have been—for him. As for me...*

Would she really be ready to wipe out the memories she had left, sweet memories of affection and laughter before it all went wrong?

'Helen?'

She came back to reality to realise that Lorenzo was staring at her. 'I asked you how the hotel was going. But you were in a daze.'

'It's the fire,' she said quickly. 'The warmth is sending me to sleep. The hotel is fine. I seem to spend my days chasing workmen, but it'll all be done in time. How did your Spanish trip go?'

'Very well. Even Renato is pleased with me, and he doesn't throw praise around.'

In this way they managed to get a very reasonable conversation going for about half an hour. It was astonishing, Helen realised, how much meaningless talk two people could indulge in without once touching the bitter reality that lay between them.

'I should be going,' she said at last.

'Yes, the light's fading,' Lorenzo agreed, handing the baby back to Angie. 'May I give you a lift?'

Helen hesitated. To refuse would be churlish. And if she insisted on Bernardo taking her he would also have to drive back up the mountain in the dark and the gathering snow.

'Thank you,' she said.

Bernardo saw them out to Lorenzo's car and waved them off before going back to his wife who was getting ready to feed the baby.

'It was nice of you to bring Helen,' she remarked placidly as she settled the infant.

'Yes, it was a lucky chance bumping into her,' he agreed.

'Did you happen to remember that Lorenzo would be here?'

He shrugged with elaborate casualness. 'It may have crossed my mind.'

'You're a devious schemer,' she chuckled.

'That's right, I am. Do you think we'll bring it off?'

'If we don't, it won't be for want of trying.'

For a while the winding mountain road took up all Lorenzo's attention, so the silence was natural. Sometimes Helen stole a glance at his profile, then looked away quickly before he could notice her. It hurt her to see the weary sadness that seemed a part of him now. As the road straightened out she said, for something to say, 'It's not like me to take an afternoon off. I shall have to make up for it this evening.'

'How are the plans going for the grand opening?' he asked politely.

'Not well. I still don't have the big idea.'

'You should call your friend Frank, the one you told me about in New York, with all the show business connections.'

'Good heavens, I never thought of Frank,' she said. 'He knows people in the movies too.'

'You need a celebrity birthday,' Lorenzo advised. 'Tell them to come and have the party here, and the Elroy will lay it on for free.'

'Of course! Where are my wits? I'll start work on it as soon as get back. We're nearly there—hey, this is the wrong turning.'

'It's the right turning for where I'm going,' he said calmly. 'There's a little place just up here, owned by a friend of mine, where we can talk.'

He parked the car, helped her out with impersonal hands, and led her to a café by a square where the trees had been hung with lights. Now they had left the mountain snow behind it was still just about warm enough to sit outside.

'What did you want to talk about?' she asked, when Lorenzo's friend had brought them almond biscuits and *prosecco*, the light, sparkling wine that Italians drink on all occasions.

'Christmas,' he said. 'Mamma wants you to come to us. She minds a lot that you haven't been to see her.'

'But how can I?'

'Your quarrel is with me, not her.'

'I have no quarrel with you, Lorenzo. How could I have when you've been good to me?'

'I'm just putting right the wrong I did you,' he said quickly.

'Heather came to see me,' she said impulsively. 'She told me what really happened.'

'She told you what I should have told you from the start. Let's not argue about whose fault it really was. We know the truth. I was afraid to tell you because I was scared you'd think me "faithless and unreliable" and I'd lose you. I brought it on myself.'

'But you must have known I'd find out,' she said. 'What did you think—?'

'Helen, have you known me all this time without realising that I don't *think*? I'm not a long-term planner like Renato, or a man who calculates details like Bernardo. I fly. Then I crash to earth and survey the wreckage and wish I'd done a bit of thinking in the first place.'

'I'm not sure you're still like that, Lorenzo.'

'Well, it's true I've been taking a hard look at myself recently. I'm not pleased with what I've seen.'

'Don't change too much,' she said impulsively. 'You wouldn't be you if you became earthbound.'

He didn't answer and she realised that he was looking at something over her shoulder. A gang of young men were regarding them with fascination. At the same moment they all raised their hands to make horns, as Giorgio had done when he left. The sign of the cuckold. Then they burst into raucous laughter.

Lorenzo put his hand firmly on hers. 'Ignore them,' he said calmly. 'Just smile and talk, but never weaken. Don't give them that satisfaction.'

Someone had started playing an accordion under trees, and a few couples were dancing. Lorenzo took her hand and got to his feet.

'Come along,' he said firmly. 'Let's really make their eyes pop.'

'You can't dance with me,' she said, scandalised.

'Just try and stop me.'

It was unnerving to be in his arms again, twisting and turning to the music, trying not to be aware of him as a thrilling male entity. Pretending, as she had always been.

'I don't know how you can do this,' she said in a low voice. 'I'm strung up the whole time.'

'You can do it because I'm here to help you.'

How kind his eyes were. In the past she'd seen them wicked and sparkling, but now it was their quiet kindness that struck her most.

'It must be worse for you,' she said. 'Do you imagine I don't know what that gesture means? Do they really think I left you for another man?'

'They don't know how to think,' he said lightly. 'I know that crowd. Tonio, Enrico, Carlo, Franco, Mario. I used to fight with most of them when I was at school. They're ignorant and they have nothing better to do.'

'They despise you for putting up with it, don't they?' she demanded hotly. 'So why do you?'

'Hey, c'mon, I'm big enough and ugly enough to look after myself.'

He gave her a grin of reassurance as though he was on top of the world, just like the old, boyish Lorenzo. But she would never see him like that again.

He'd said 'ugly', but he wasn't ugly. He was handsome enough to have any woman he wanted, but he chose to be here, protecting a woman who'd insulted him, exposing himself to derision, because he believed she needed his help and support. Her eyes pricked.

'Don't cry,' Lorenzo said frantically. 'What will people think?'

'They'll think you're having a go at me, and respect you for it,' she said, hastily blowing her nose.

'Stuff that! Do you think I want their good opinion at your expense? Act as if everything's normal between us.'

'I'm not sure what that means,' Helen said, pulling herself together. 'What is "normal between us"? We've always been playing parts, right from the start when we were just going to be friends.'

He gave a grunt of laughter. 'I used to take cold showers every night, just thinking of you.'

'That's what I mean. We've never been honest with each other about anything.'

'I suppose that's true,' he mused. 'Perhaps it's time we started.'

Something in his tone made her look up to discover his mouth close to hers. He brushed her lips lightly, but did no more, watching for her reaction.

'That wasn't wise,' she said in shaking voice.

'It was honest,' he said. 'And I wanted to do it.'

'But you said—'

'What did I say?' he whispered, so close that his breath touched her face.

'I forget.'

Their lips were touching again and joy seemed to stream through her as though a window had opened onto sunlight. She had been so unhappy, and now it seemed as though everything might be given back to her. This time she would know how to protect and treasure it.

'Come back to the villa,' he murmured. 'There's so much we must talk about.'

'All right.'

He led her back to the table. While she was gathering her things Helen was vaguely aware of Lorenzo lifting a paper that had been slipped under his wine glass. When she looked at him he was staring at it, frozen. She reached for it too quickly for him to stop her.

It was a swiftly drawn sketch, crude but effective, of a woman walking a poodle on a leash. The woman's face was just recognisable as her own, while Lorenzo's face had been substituted for the poodle's.

'That's what they think of you because you act like a civilised human being?' she raged. 'And you ask what I've always held against this place. Doesn't this explain it?'

He was deadly pale. 'It doesn't matter. I care nothing for them beside—' He checked himself.

'I'm not going to let this happen again, Lorenzo. I won't accept a sacrifice. Please tell your mother that I'm sorry I can't come over

Christmas. In fact, I can't see you again, ever. Can't you understand that I *mustn't*?'

He didn't try to prevent her leaving. Just watched her go with a face that was dark with anger, and tore the paper into shreds.

CHAPTER ELEVEN

THE Elroy-Palermo opened in a blaze of glory. Helen's call to Frank had produced the goods in the form of a pair of Hollywood starlets about to tie the knot. After some negotiations they married in Palermo and held the reception at the hotel, courtesy of Elroys. The pictures were glorious and they appeared in magazines all over the world. Helen also managed a nifty deal on video rights, providing herself with the perfect publicity weapon.

'Well done,' Lorenzo said, taking her aside at the reception. 'You've made a brilliant success.'

'I didn't know you were going to be here.'

'It should have been Renato but I persuaded him to let me come instead. It was the only way I could get to see you since you're avoiding us.'

'I'm not—'

'You wouldn't come for Christmas, you wouldn't join us for the christening in the cathedral. They named Bernardo and Angie's baby Marta, by the way. After his mother. The whole family was there except you.'

'How could I come, knowing what happens to you if we're seen together? Or even if we're not.'

'That's all over.'

'You mean that crowd of punks don't bother you any more?'

'Of course not. They've lost interest.'

'Lorenzo, I hear all the gossip in this place.'

'And the gossip features me, does it?' He spoke casually but she could see his chagrin.

'In neon lights.'

'It's been two months since we saw each other,' he growled. 'You'd think they'd find something better to talk about.'

'I'll bet they send you things in the mail too, don't they?' He shrugged. 'Oh, it's unspeakable!' she snapped. 'Why don't you do something to stop them?'

'Like what?' he demanded.

'How should I know?'

'Are we back to the blood feud again? My father had an old shotgun somewhere. I could look it out if you think my dignity demands it.

Only I've never used it before, and if I aimed it at you I'd probably miss and break Mamma's best vase, and then she'd get mad at me and—'

'Not as mad as I'm getting. Why can't you take it seriously?'

'Because I can't keep a straight face when you talk that *vendetta* nonsense. You're a real hot-blooded Sicilian, aren't you? You terrify me. Why don't you get the shotgun if you're so determined on action?'

She ground her teeth. 'There's no point in me taking action when you're the one with the cause for a *vendetta*.'

He made a wry face. 'I'm sorry, Helen. I guess I must be a real disappointment to you.'

There was no way past the shield he put up against her arrows. She recalled Heather saying how he'd once taken a tipsy swing at a British policeman. But that had been another Lorenzo. This was a man so rock-solid in his knowledge of, and confidence in, himself, that he could endure smarts that would destroy a lesser man.

She felt a sudden dread at the thought that he wasn't doing this for her at all. Perhaps he was simply proving something to himself, and she was almost irrelevant. It hurt far more than it should have done.

She would have returned to the battle, but he drifted away, calling, 'Congratulations on a great day,' over his shoulder.

This so incensed Helen that the next day, with the praises of Head Office ringing in her ears, she fled the hotel, jumped into her car and drove out to the Residenza, just as she'd promised herself she would never do.

'There's no doing anything with him,' she said stormily when Baptista had greeted her with pleasure, and settled her down on the sofa. 'He's totally unreasonable.'

'I'm afraid he is,' Baptista agreed.

'He can't talk sense about anything.'

'He's never been able to.'

'And when it concerns me, he's completely off his head.'

'Since the day he met you, my dear,' Baptista agreed placidly. 'He tried to hide it, but I knew at once that "Elena" was special.'

'He doesn't call me Elena now,' Helen said sadly. 'It used to make me angry, but now I've realised that he called me that when he loved me. Now I'm just Helen.'

'Which is what you wanted,' Baptista observed.

'It was what I wanted *then*. I hadn't understood a lot of things—then.'

'And that is the beginning of wisdom.'

'What's the point of my being wise now?' Helen asked passionately. 'When it's too late. When I think of what he's going through—'

'Some stories reach me. He tells me nothing.'

'The things that come in his mail—no, of course, he wouldn't show you.'

'His mail doesn't come here. Lorenzo doesn't live in this house any more. He moved out to the villa weeks ago.'

'The villa? He lives there—alone?'

'He has no other woman, my dear.'

She hadn't been thinking of that. What hurt was the thought of Lorenzo alone in the house where they had planned to share love. Alone. Waking up alone. Going to bed alone. Lorenzo, a man who liked to be with people.

'You really don't understand him, do you?' Baptista asked.

'No. I used to think he was uncomplicated and easy to understand. But now he's shut me out of his mind and I can't follow any of his thoughts.'

'It's really very simple. This is still a very old-fashioned society where men and women are concerned. A man's pride should matter to him more than anything else, more than any woman. As people see it, you insulted Lorenzo and he should avenge his honour. But he does not. Instead he champions and protects a woman who has publicly scorned him. And so they deride him as a fool.'

'It's so unjust, both to me and to him.'

'True. But a man who shows that a woman matters more to him than anything else in life has a hard road to travel.'

'Love,' Helen mused wistfully. 'I can't hope that he still loves me.'

'If he doesn't, why do you think he endures humiliation for you?' Baptista demanded, a little sternly. 'Don't question his feelings. Question your own. Lorenzo has sacrificed his pride for your sake. By doing so he has set you above his home, his rearing, his family, his country. *Miu fighia*, it's a great responsibility when a man loves you as much as that. Even a great burden. Are you strong enough for such a burden?'

'Yes,' Helen said decisively. 'I thought I loved him before, but the feelings I had then look so shallow. Now, when he's so strong and kind, caring for me without complaining or reproaching me, I've come to see him as a man I can admire and respect as well as love. Why, that was it,' she said in a tone of discovery. 'There was always something missing before, and that was it.'

'And now it's in place,' Baptista said. 'So you will know what to do.'

The little hotel stood in the heart of Palermo, its best room looking out directly onto the main square and its colourful life. From the window of that room Helen could judge her moment precisely.

She'd rented it three days ago, knowing that she would have to be patient, but also knowing that she wasn't struggling alone. Angie and Heather were on her side, and both had given their husbands careful instructions. Baptista too had been involved in the organisation, which had prompted her to reminisce about how she had arranged Heather and Renato's wedding, and the role she had played in Angie and Bernardo's. She had ended by observing tartly that however clever her sons thought they were, none of them seemed capable of getting married without their mother's help. Whereupon the four women had cracked open a bottle of champagne to toast each other.

Now the evening was here and everything was in place. She'd persuaded the baffled hotelier to bring up a small table to stand just to the side of the window, and a lamp to put on it. She made him shift them twice before she was completely satisfied, and then he fled downstairs to tell his wife that their guest was crazy.

She was wearing the dark red silk dress from the night they met, and her black hair was hanging about her shoulders. She usually wore it up these days, but tonight she cast aside her business self and became simply a woman with a man in her sights.

Spring hadn't properly begun, but in Palermo the climate was mild and many bars and cafes had tables out in the open. There was one just below her, at right angles to her corner room, so that she could see the tables clearly.

The next moment Renato appeared, his hand resting on Lorenzo's shoulder. He indicated a seat on the pavement, apparently suggesting that they sit here and have a drink. Lorenzo shrugged and sat down while Renato summoned the waiter and ordered drinks.

Well and good. The first of her allies was doing his part. Now all it needed was the second….

And there was Bernardo, right on cue, strolling into the square from a side street, accompanied by a little crowd of young men. Lorenzo looked up, and even from here Helen could discern his surprise at the company his brother kept. For there were Tonio and Enrico, Carlo, Franco and Mario—all Lorenzo's tormentors. And Bernardo, the least sociable man in the world, was laughing with them, inviting them to sit down and drink at his expense, which they were eager to do. He even directed them to seats where they and Lorenzo had a clear view of each other.

Helen gave a little murmur of satisfaction. Bernardo's role was the hardest but he was doing it perfectly.

'You leave it to me,' he'd said only yester-day. 'I'll round that scum up and deliver them just where and when you need them.'

So now everything was ready for her. All she had to do was step out into that square, play the part she'd set herself, and trust to Lorenzo's reaction. Her heart almost failed her when she thought what that might be. Would he understand? Would he respond?

But even if it didn't, she would have re-stored his dignity in the face of all Palermo, and that was worth any sacrifice.

She switched the table lamp on and pulled the curtains apart so that anyone standing be-low would have a good view of the window and just a little way inside. That was an essen-tial part of her plan. Then, taking a deep breath, she left the room, went down the stairs and out into the square.

Lorenzo didn't see her at first, but before she had crossed the short distance that separated them something made him aware of her. He raised his head from his wine glass and be-came very still as she strolled the last few feet to stand in front of him. She moved almost casually, deliberately unhurried, so that nobody should guess that her heart was thumping and her mouth was dry with apprehension. All around them a silence gradually fell. Lorenzo's tormentors were watching closely, avid for any new ammunition.

Helen let them look, giving them time to take in her rich beauty and the fact that she'd come prepared for the fray. Lorenzo frowned a little, as though wondering why she'd chosen to confront him in these circumstances. In return for his frown she gave him a slow, luxuriant smile, implicit with a promise that no man could have misunderstood.

'Did you want something with me?' Lorenzo asked, puzzled and cautious.

'Yes,' she said in a clear voice. 'I do.'

She didn't move. She waited for him to rise and come to her. Very slowly he did so, standing close and looking into her eyes.

'What can I do for you?' he asked gently.

'This,' she said, drawing him quickly towards her with a movement that wasn't gentle at all. She was kissing him before he had time to think, wrapping her arms about his neck, her fingers in his hair in a theatrical parade of seduction, and all the time she was praying that he would understand.

He didn't kiss her back at once, but that was all right, she told herself. The point was to tell the world that *she* wanted *him*. So she put everything she had into it, enticing him with her lips and her hands, assaulting his senses so that they would yield before he could think straight.

She let her fingertips play on the back of his neck and felt the jolt that went through him. She was reminding him of memories he'd spent months suppressing, using all her strength, all the allure of which she was capable, to make him remember, and long for her. And the power of his arms about her told her that she was succeeding.

He was taking over the kiss, and she gladly let him do so, for his lips were caressing hers with an urgency she hadn't dared to hope for again. He'd longed for her as much as she had done for him, and now anything was possible. Which meant the time had come for the next part of her plan.

She gently released herself and stepped back.

'Is that all you wanted?' he asked, watching her intently, beginning to understand, but not daring to hope…

'No, it's not all.' She took a deep breath. Her heart was pounding at the risk she was taking, but nothing was going to stop her now. 'I want you to go with me to the cathedral—and marry me,' she said in a voice loud enough to be heard by them all. 'Do you understand, Lorenzo? I want to marry you.'

His brows drew together a little. 'Are you sure that's a good idea?' he murmured.

'Yes,' she said in the same clear voice. 'I'm quite sure it's a good idea.' She took his hand. 'Come with me, and I'll show you just how good an idea it is.'

She began to walk in the direction of the hotel, moving languidly, but actually keeping his hand firmly clasped in hers. She knew now that he wouldn't reject her in public. He'd divined part of her intention, but only a part, she thought with a small, private smile.

He followed her up the narrow stairs to the room she'd rented, and inside. She still held his hand, and when she'd locked the door she drew him over to the window where they would be in full view of the square. As she had hoped a little crowd had gathered below. Tonio, Enrico and the others were there, with Renato and Bernardo bringing up the rear, like shepherds corralling the sheep into place. As they appeared in the window a burst of applause floated up, which intensified as they went into each other's arms.

'I don't want to kiss you in front of a crowd,' he said.

'But you need to. You need them to know that I'm yours—in any way you want.'

'Do you think I care about them—or anything beside you?'

She touched his face. 'I know. But we had to show them—together. Pull the curtains.' He did so and a cheer reached them. 'Now put out the light,' she whispered against his lips. 'It's there on the table, beside your hand.'

'You had it all planned, didn't you?'

'Right down to the last detail.'

He switched out the little table lamp and the sudden darkness brought another cheer, louder than ever. But neither of them heard it. She was already working on his buttons.

'Elena, are you sure this is what you want to do?'

'Hush,' she murmured, brushing her finger-tips over his lips. 'We have unfinished business.'

After that he had nothing more to say. As she finished his buttons he stood watching her with eyes full of love, then pulled the shirt off himself, and tossed it aside.

'Your move,' he said.

She laughed softly and ran her fingers tips lightly over his chest. Oh yes, she thought, feeling his trembling response. *Oh, yes!*

'Elena—Helen—'

'This is Elena,' she assured him.

Helen was the cool, calculating woman who had measured her love to see how much it was wise to give. Elena was ready to give every-thing without counting the cost. From now on she would always be Elena. She drew him close so that she could rest her face against his neck, close her eyes and make the world van-ish. In the darkness there must be only the two of them.

His fingers were working at the back of the red dress. It took only a moment to be rid of it, and his eyes widened with delight as he realised that she wore nothing at all underneath.

'Why, you cheeky little—'

'I was very determined to have you,' she said. 'Don't keep me waiting.'

She was in his arms before the words were out, lifted high against his broad chest and carried to the waiting bed. Then they were lying together, her body against his, discovering each other. Looking at Lorenzo now she wondered how she could ever have doubted that he still wanted her. There was no mistaking the urgency of his desire. It was there too in the hands that shook as they touched her. She drew him gently over her, silently offering him everything she had, or was, or would ever be. And he accepted with passionate love and gratitude.

As he looked at her face on the pillow, her black hair spread out in disarray, he had a brief glimpse of the woman he'd met a year ago, tense, confused, hiding her uneasiness with courage and laughter. But he'd seen beneath them to her vulnerability, and it had made him all hers long before he knew it. Now, as he felt her moving against him, he knew that the pact was mutual: gift for gift, love for love, life for life.

Afterwards she sat beside him on the bed, gently stroking his body and observing the signs that his desire was mounting again.

'You haven't answered me,' she reminded him.

'About what, *carissima*?'

'I asked if you would marry me.'

He kissed her fingers. 'There's nothing I want more in the world than to marry you— Elena.'

CHAPTER TWELVE

THE ravishing dress gleamed as Helen twisted and turned before the bedroom mirror, trying to see herself from all angles.

'You look gorgeous,' Heather said, gently lifting the veil. Helen bent her head while her two matrons of honour set it in place and fixed it with the tiara.

'Is it secure?' she asked anxiously.

'Completely safe,' Angie assured her.

'Do you think I should have chosen a different dress? Perhaps it's bad luck to wear the same one as last time—'

'Stop getting paranoid,' Heather told her firmly. 'This is the dress for your wedding to Lorenzo. It's been a bit delayed, but it's the same wedding, and everything about it should be the same.'

'Well, not quite *everything*,' Angie said quickly. The three of them laughed a little nervously.

'But all the other details are the same,' Heather said. 'Poor little Vanzini has been rehearsing the *Jubilate* until everyone's going crazy. He's determined that nothing's going to stop him this time.'

There was a knock on the door and Helen's father looked in. 'The cars are here,' he said.

Angie and Heather, who were going in the first car, kissed Helen and departed in a flutter of blue silk.

Nicolo came to stand in front of his daughter. 'No doubts this time?' he asked kindly.

'No doubts, Poppa. I was never more certain of anything in my life.'

'Then shall we go?'

'Yes—no—where's your flower?'

Aghast, he stared at his buttonhole. 'I'm sure your mother gave me one. It must still be in my room.'

'Hurry.'

He sped away. While she waited for him Helen strolled out onto the wide terrace and looked out over the countryside. Everywhere she saw the green of spring, glowing under the early sun. It was the perfect time to start a new life with the man she loved. As she'd told Poppa, this time she was quite certain.

She was so entranced at the view that she came to herself with a start, realising that some time had passed. Nicolo dashed in, looking flustered, but with a flower in his buttonhole.

'It's your Mamma's fault,' he declared in answer to her look. 'She'd hidden it.'

'Poppa! Of course she hadn't hidden it.'

'Well, I couldn't find it.'

'We'd better hurry.'

He escorted her out to where the car was standing, its door held open by Guido, the new chauffeur, very young and proud to bursting of his uniform and responsibilities. He explained that the other car had left several minutes previously.

'Step on it,' Nicolo commanded the driver as they settled in the back.

In a moment they'd swung out of the courtyard, through the tiny village that nestled at the foot of the incline, and out into the open country. Helen looked worriedly out of the window.

'We've got plenty of time,' Nicolo said. 'Every bride is a little late.'

'Not this bride,' Helen said fervently. 'After last time I can't afford to be late by so much as a second. Think of what it would put him through.'

A glance at her watch showed that they had made up a little time. She began to relax. She was thinking ahead to Lorenzo in the cathedral, waiting for her, flanked by his brothers. Memories of last time would make him nervous. He would worry in case she wasn't coming at all. Then he would dismiss his fears as superstition, but he would worry nonetheless, staring down the long aisle to catch the first glimpse of her.

She pictured his face as she appeared. She would smile to reassure him that all was well. And then their life together would begin.

Suddenly she was thrown sideways.

'What's happened?' she gasped.

The car had reached the crest of a hill and skidded slightly. The driver fought to regain control but it was useless. The great vehicle drifted, almost elegantly, to the side of the road, and deposited itself nose down in a ditch.

'Oh no!' Helen wailed. 'This can't be happening.'

She scrambled out and looked up and down the road, but they were out in the country and there was nobody to be seen. From this height she could just see the other car vanishing into the distance. She waved and shouted, but she knew they wouldn't hear her.

Lorenzo was waiting for her. Soon he would be wondering why she was late, thinking himself abandoned again.

'The phone,' she said urgently. 'We can call his mobile.'

Guido lunged for the car phone, but Lorenzo's mobile was switched off. So was Bernardo's.

'Try Renato,' Helen said tensely. 'He *never* turns his mobile off.'

But the dawning look of dismay on Guido's face as he dialled and listened told her that she was unlucky again.

'Now I remember Signor Renato has changed his number,' he said wretchedly. 'I don't have the new number.'

Nicolo prepared to lash himself into a temper. 'It's your job to keep up with these things,' he roared.

'That's enough, Poppa,' Helen said quickly. 'It's not his fault, he's new at the job.'

'But I insist—'

'Poppa, let it go.' Helen spoke too absently to notice the astonishment on her father's face. 'We have more important things to think of. I've got to get to Palermo.'

'How? Fly?'

'No, there's some transport coming now.'

He followed her pointing finger to where a vehicle had appeared over the hill.

'That's a pig cart,' Nicolo said in outrage. 'And it's being drawn by a mule.'

'It's got wheels,' Helen said firmly. 'It can get me there.'

She placed herself firmly in the middle of the road and hailed the cart. The old man driving it halted his aged mule and looked down at her, his oaken face betraying no surprise at being stopped by a bride in the middle of nowhere.

'I have to get to Palermo cathedral,' Helen said urgently. 'You see—'

'Yes, I see,' said the man, taking in the ditched car in a glance. 'I would help you but I have no room.' He jerked his head over his shoulder at where the four pigs took up all the space. 'I'm taking them to market.'

'I'll buy them,' Helen said quickly. 'Here and now. How much?'

He named a price. Nicolo gave an indignant yelp.

'It's too much. I buy pigs like that every day for half the price.'

'Then you take the bride,' the driver said cunningly.

Helen became businesslike. 'Poppa, how much is fair?' He told her and she turned back to the driver. 'We split the difference.'

He began to argue. She argued back. For the first time in her life Helen was glad she spoke Sicilian, for nothing else would have served her now. She was afraid her father would interrupt, but he was staring at her as though he'd never seen her before.

At last they agreed a price. But there was still a snag. Only Guido was carrying money, and he didn't have enough. The driver lifted his reins and prepared to drive on.

'No,' Helen said fiercely. 'You're not moving a step. I'll double your original price—'

'Without money? How?'

'I'll give you my note of hand.'

'Hah!'

'It will be honoured. Do you think you can't trust a note from *Signora Elena Martelli*?'

He stared at her. 'You are a Martelli?'

'I will be when you've moved those pigs and taken me to Palermo.'

The driver tossed the reins to Guido, jumped down and went to the end of the cart.

'Guido I'm afraid you're going to have to stay here,' Helen said, looking about her, 'with the livestock.'

'No problem,' he said. 'I'll call a garage to rescue the car, then a friend of mine who has a farm.'

'Fine. Take good care of my pigs. I'm going to give them to my husband as a wedding present.'

At last the back of the cart was empty. Guido went to the car, returning with a note pad and pen, and a blanket. While Helen scribbled her note of hand he spread out the blanket where the pigs had been.

'Now your dress stays clean,' he said, assisting her into the back.

'Thank you, Guido. Poppa, come on.'

Her father was regarding her aghast. 'Me?' he roared. 'You expect me to travel in that?'

'You've got to give me away.'

'If the family finds out I'll never live it down.'

'Well they won't,' she said exasperated. 'I promise not to tell Aunt Lucia in Maryland, so she can't tell Aunt Zita in Idaho, and *she* can't tell Aunt Clarrie in Los Angeles. Now, Poppa, *quit arguing and get into the cart.*'

He stared. 'What did you say to your Poppa?'

'I said get into the cart, and I meant it. I'm going to be there to marry Lorenzo, and you're going to be there to give me away.'

'Stop looking nervous,' Renato advised his brother. 'She'll be here at any moment.'

'She should have been here five minutes ago,' Lorenzo said worriedly. 'Bernardo, go and check.'

'I've just got back from checking. Angie
and Heather are here and they say Helen was
following just behind.'

'Then where is she?'

'She'll be here,' Renato assured him.
'Look, I know what you're thinking, and forget it. Elena is a honest woman. If she was
going to stand you up she wouldn't just van-
ish. She'd come here and say so.'

Lorenzo turned appalled eyes on him and
Bernardo muttered, 'You might have put that
better.'

Lorenzo tried to shut out the sound of their
voices, and the consciousness that the congregation was getting restless. He knew what
they were thinking and he wanted to shout at
them that they were wrong. His Elena loved
him, and wouldn't do this to him. It was different from last time. Now, as well as love,
they had trust and understanding.

But as the minutes ticked past with no sign
of her his dread grew, and his future appeared
before him—a blank of misery, because the
woman he loved had abandoned him in the
most callous way imaginable.

'What was that?' Renato asked suddenly.

Lorenzo forced himself back to reality. 'What?'

'I thought I heard cheering.'

'So did I,' Bernardo said. 'And applause. Somewhere outside. I'm going to see.'

He almost ran down the aisle and found his wife hurrying towards him, almost dancing in her excitement. 'Come quickly,' she said, grasping his hand.

At the cathedral door Bernardo took one look at the incredible sight before dashing back and roaring down the length of the cathedral, *'Lorenzo, come and look at this!'*

Then, not only Lorenzo, but half the congregation was on the move, hurrying out into the sunshine, adding their cheers to the crowd when they saw what was happening. Even the choir hurried out and began hollering and dancing with glee.

A vehicle was approaching down the length of the Corso Vittorio Emanuele, and attracting a good deal of attention. Traffic was halting, drivers leaning out and cheering, policeman grinned and waved the vehicle through, while crowds of smiling people lined the road.

'If I'm not very much mistaken,' Renato said, 'that's Enrico Cacelli's pig cart.'

'And in the back....' Bernardo said.

'Yes,' Lorenzo said in a daze. 'In the back....'

'Any other woman,' Renato observed, 'goes to her wedding in a car.'

A smile was breaking over Lorenzo's face. 'But my Elena is like no other woman in the world.'

The bride saw him and waved frantically. As the cart rumbled into the piazza he began to run. Enrico Cacelli drew the mule to a halt so suddenly that Helen almost tumbled out of the back, into Lorenzo's arms.

'The car—' she began, and the rest was cut off by his mouth. When she could speak again she said breathlessly, 'I was so afraid you'd think I wasn't coming.'

'I never doubted you for one moment,' Lorenzo said emphatically. He lifted her high in strong arms. 'Now,' he said firmly, 'we go to church, and I'm not letting go of you until you're Signora Martelli.'

'That's all I want to be,' she assured him joyfully.

'Then let's go.'

The crowd cheered and applauded, the choir burst into the *Jubilate*, and the sound followed Lorenzo Martelli and Elena Angolini into the cathedral for the wedding that had waited too long.

MILLS & BOON® PUBLISH EIGHT LARGE PRINT TITLES A MONTH. THESE ARE THE EIGHT TITLES FOR MAY 2002

MILLS & BOON®

Makes any time special™

MILLS & BOON® PUBLISH EIGHT LARGE PRINT TITLES A MONTH. THESE ARE THE EIGHT TITLES FOR JUNE 2002

A SECRET VENGEANCE
Miranda Lee

THE ITALIAN'S BRIDE
Diana Hamilton

D'ALESSANDRO'S CHILD
Catherine Spencer

DESERT AFFAIR
Kate Walker

THE ENGAGEMENT EFFECT
Neels & Fielding

THE ENGLISHMAN'S BRIDE
Sophie Weston

THE BRIDEGROOM'S VOW
Rebecca Winters

THE WEDDING DARE
Barbara Hannay

MILLS & BOON®

Makes any time special™